ALASKA STORIES

TALES FROM THE LAST FRONTIER

EDITED BY JOHN AND KIRSTEN MILLER

CHRONICLE BOOKS

SAN FRANCISCO

Printed in the United States of America.

Library of Congress Cataloging-in-Publication Data:

Alaska stories : tales from the last frontier /
edited by John and Kirsten Miller.
p.   cm.
ISBN 0-8118-0675-8 (pbk.)
1. Frontier and pioneer life—Alaska—Literary collections.
2. Frontier and pioneer life—Alaska. 3. Alaska—Social life
and customs. 4. American literature—Alaska.
I. Miller, John, 1959- . II. Miller, Kirsten, 1962- .
PS571.A4A43 1995
813.009'32798—dc20   94-15574
CIP

Book and cover design: Big Fish Books
Compostition: Jennifer Petersen, Big Fish Books
Cover Photograph: Fred Hirschmann

Distributed in Canada by Raincoast Books,
8680 Cambie Street, Vancouver, B.C. V6P 6M9

10 9 8 7 6 5 4 3 2 1

Chronicle Books
275 Fifth Street
San Francisco, CA 94103

Special Thanks to Larry Gallagher

and Michael Doogan

Contents

MICHAEL DOOGAN

Introduction

PEOPLE EXPECT A lot of Alaska. Always have. Writers encourage them to.

They come looking for things they don't have. Challenge. Money. Danger. Fresh air. Some find what they're looking for. Some don't. But the writers always discover myths.

William Dall and John McPhee found The Wilderness. Emily Craig Romig and Larry Gallagher found The Frontier. Jack London and Alistair Scott found Adventure. Alaska is the big, unsettled corner where

---

Born-and-bred Alaskan Michael Doogan has spent the last ten years writing for the Anchorage Daily News, *where he contributes a thrice-a-week metro column. He also writes regularly for* Alaska *magazine.*

the myths no longer useful in modern America ended up.

Myths are fine subjects for writers, but they make difficult neighbors. They were not kind to my forefathers, who were drawn to Alaska by Opportunity.

"Papa says he is not going to leave here until he gets a barrel of money," my great-uncle Willie Feero wrote from Skagway in 1897. My great-grandfather, John, ran a pack train over the White Pass trail during the Klondike gold rush. He did not get a barrel of money, but he didn't leave, either. He fell ill and froze to death between Skagway and Lake Bennett. At fifteen, Willie Feero became the man of his family.

Those are my mother's people. My father's parents arrived in Juneau 15 years later. My grandfather, Teague, worked in the stamp mills of gold mines. The dust ate up his lungs, and he died of miner's pneumonia. At sixteen, my father became the man of his family.

Living among myths has gotten easier, but not easy. At the age of ten or eleven, I was sent out with several dozen other boys into the stone-cold heart of interior Alaska's winter. We built spruce bough lean-tos, hacked fire pits in the frozen ground and endured temperatures of fifty below zero. We were Boy Scouts. This was winter survival training. An Adventure in The Wilderness. If I'd had a Jack London novel, I'd have used it to build a fire.

At about the same time, I began helping my father deliver coal to the tiny cabins of Fairbanks. I climbed down into their small, pitch-black coal bins. Coal poured in. I shoveled it frantically to the sides, trying to keep the only opening clear. When the job was finished, I crawled out into the frigid air and spit coal dust into the snow. In this way, a bin could be made to hold enough coal for two weeks' use. Life on The Frontier could go on.

Unlike my forefathers, I was not killed by the cold or the dust. But I am a third-generation Alaskan. You might say I have a certain, genetic skepticism of myths.

Which is not the same thing as being able to ignore them.

The Frontier does invade The Wilderness. Sometimes, it leaves scars.

North of Fairbanks, tailing piles mark the routes of the big gold dredges, boats full of machinery that ate up the countryside and spit out a moonscape. I played on them as a kid.

From the air, I watched oil seep from the shattered side of the Exxon Valdez and spread across Prince William Sound like a virus.

On the banks of the Yukon River, I found a forgotten campfire burning along under the tundra, charring the trunks of black spruce and smoking mightily.

But the relationship between The Frontier and The Wilderness is not one-sided.

A moose winters in my neighborhood, sauntering down my street at odd hours. I have pictures of it in my next-door neighbor's backyard.

On a busy street a half-dozen blocks away, cars stop in early summer to let wild geese lead strings of goslings across unmolested.

Last year, or maybe the year before, a grizzly bear was killed a dozen blocks from the heart of downtown.

The Frontier and The Wilderness are not always the antagonistic forces of myth. In Alaska, civilization is not acid poured on the land, but the thinnest veneer applied to a restless landscape. Sometimes, the veneer smothers what's underneath. Mostly, though, nature is a match for the efforts of men. The Wilderness persists.

So does Adventure. I have found it myself. While loading cages of sea otters onto a cargo plane on the Aleutian island of Amchitka. Sitting lazily in a raft on the Yukon River. Bouncing around the deck of a tug in Kachemak Bay. Peering unsteadily from a seat in an after-hours joint in Kotzebue. Standing in my front yard, looking up at the shimmering, darting greens of the northern lights.

Still, myths make difficult neighbors. I sometimes think that if it were up to me, I would simply evict them all. Send them packing for some wilder place. Outer space, maybe. Alaska would be quieter then, no longer full of people striving so noisily to protect one myth from the others. Trying to save The Wilderness from The Frontier. Trying to push The Frontier a little farther into The Wilderness.

But then this wouldn't be Alaska anymore. So instead of banishing the myths, I think I'll just try to deal with them in smaller pieces. Story-sized pieces, like the ones in this book. A bit of The Wilderness here. A chunk of The Frontier there. A slice of Adventure that would fit in the palm of your hand.

Like the one I found flying out of Denali National Park. I'd driven in with the governor and the secretary of Interior, listening to the governor explain the needs of The Frontier and the Secretary expound on the rights of The Wilderness. We saw moose and bear and caribou, but the drive along the 90-mile park road was as adventurous as a day of watching C-SPAN.

The flight out was a different story. The alpine tundra was on fire with the reds and yellows of fall. Game trails led in every direction. In the valleys ran rivers born at the faces of glaciers. On the shoulder of a high ridge, in a sloping bowl, grazed more than a dozen of the shy, bone-white sheep named for William Dall. As the pilot banked to get a better view, the unseen currents of the air, chopped and channeled by the peaks and valleys, tossed the little airplane sharply this way and that. There was, as there often is, beauty at the intersection of The Frontier and The Wilderness. And a little danger.

But just a little.

JOHN MCPHEE

The Encircled River

7 A.M., AND THE water temperature is forty-four, the air fifty-six, the sky blue and clear—an Indian-summer morning, August 18, 1975. Pourchot, after breakfast, goes off to measure the largest of the spruce near the campsite. He finds a tree twenty-two inches in diameter, breast high. Most of the spruce in this country look like pipe cleaners. The better ones look like bottle washers. Tough they may be, but they are on the edge of their world, and their trucks can grow fifty years and be scarcely an inch through. Yet here is a stand of trees a foot thick. A specimen nearly two. Pourchot says he will write in his report that there is *one* tree of such girth.

John McPhee's New Yorker *essays have been collected in several varied volumes, including* The Survival of the Bark Canoe, Oranges, *and* The Curve of Binding Energy *(about the atomic bomb). But McPhee is in top form when writing about the wild, as in his classic 1977 Alaska adventure,* Coming into the Country.

"Otherwise, the Forest Service might think there's timber here."

Two of our boats—the kayaks—are German. They can be taken apart and put back together. They were invented long ago by someone known as the Mad Tailor of Rosenheim. The Mad Tailor, at the turn of the century, was famous for his mountain-climbing knickers and loden capes. It was in 1907 that he went into naval architecture on a diminutive scale. Every major valley in Bavaria had a railroad running through it. The forests were laced with small white rivers. It was all but impossible to get boats to them, because boats were too bulky to accompany travellers on trains. Wouldn't it be *phantastisch*, thought the tailor, if a boat could fit into a handbag, if a suitcase could turn into a kayak? His name was Johann Klepper. He designed a collapsible kayak with a canvas skin and a frame of separable hardwood parts. In subsequent manufacture, the boat became an international success. Klepper might have stopped there. Not long after the First World War, he designed a larger version, its spray cover apertured with two holes. Where the original boat had been made for a single paddler, this one was intended for a team. We have with us a single and a double Klepper. The smaller one is prompt, responsive, feathery on the stream. The double one is somewhat less maneuverable than a three-ton log. Stell Newman, of the National Park Service, began calling it Snake Eyes, and everyone has picked up the name. Snake Eyes is our *bateau noir*, our Charonian ferry, our *Höllenfahrt*. Throughout the day, we heap opprobrium on Snake Eyes.

Pourchot and I have the double Klepper this mourning. The ratio of expended energy to develop momentum is seventy-five to one. This is in part because the bottom of Snake Eyes at times intersects the bottom of the river, which is shallow at many of the riffles. The hull has become so abraded in places that it has developed leaks. The Grumman canoe is wider, longer, more heavily loaded. It carries at least half of all our gear.

Nonetheless, it rides higher, draws less water, than Snake Eyes. Fortunately, the pools are extensive here in the lower river, and are generally a little deeper than a paddle will reach. Pockets are much deeper than that. Miles slide behind us. A salmon, sensing the inferiority of Snake Eyes, leaps into the air beside it, leaps again, leaps again, ten pounds of fish jumping five times high into the air—a bravado demonstration, a territorial declaration. This is, after all, the salmon's eponymous river. The jumper moves on, among its kind, ignoring the dying. These—their spawning done—idly, sleepily yield to the current, their gestures slow and quiet, a peaceful drifting away.

We have moved completely out of the hills now, and beyond the riverine fringes of spruce and cottonwood are boggy flatlands and thaw lakes. We see spruce that have been chewed by porcupines and cottonwood chewed by beavers. Moose tend to congregate down here on the tundra plain. In late fall, some of the caribou that migrate through the Salmon valley will stop here and make this their winter range. We see a pair of loons, and lesser Canada geese, and chick mergansers with their mother. Mink, marten, muskrat, otter—creatures that live here inhabit the North Woods across the world to Maine. We pass a small waterfall under a patterned bluff—folded striations of schist. In bends of the river now we come upon banks of flood-eroded soil—of mud. They imply an earth mantle of some depth going back who knows how far from the river. Brown and glistening, they are virtually identical with rural stream banks in the eastern half of the country, with the difference that the water flowing past these is clear. In the sixteenth century, the streams of eastern America ran clear (except in flood), but after people began taking the vegetation off the soil mantle and then leaving their fields fallow when crops were not there, rain carried the soil into streams. The process continues, and when one looks at such streams today, in their seasonal varieties of chocolate, their distant past is—even to the imagination—completely lost. For this Alaskan river, on the other hand, the sixteenth century has not yet ended, nor the fifteenth, nor the fifth. The river flows, as it has since immemorial time, in balance with itself. The river and every rill that feeds it are in an unmodified natural state—opaque in flood, ordinarily clear, with levels that change within a closed cycle of the year and of the years. The river cycle is only one of many hundreds of cycles—biological, meteorological—that coincide and blend here in the absence of intruding artifice. Past to present, present reflecting past, the cycles compose this segment of the earth. It is not static, so it cannot be styled "pristine," except in the special sense that while human beings have hunted, fished, and gathered wild food in this valley in small groups for centuries, they have not yet begun to change it. Such a description will fit many rivers in Alaska. This one, though, with its considerable beauty and a geography that places it partly within and partly beyond the extreme reach of the boreal forest, has been thought of as sufficiently splendid to become a national wild river—to be set aside with its immediate environs as unalterable wild terrain. Kauffmann, Newman, Fedeler, and Pourchot are, in their various ways, studying that possibility. The wild-river proposal, which Congress is scheduled to act upon before the end of 1978, is something of a box within a box, for it is entirely incorporated within a proposed national monument that would include not only the entire Salmon River drainage but also a large segment of the valley of the Kobuk River, of which the Salmon is a tributary. (In the blue haze of Interior Department terminology, "national monument" often enough describes certain large bodies of preserved land that in all respects except name are national parks.) The Kobuk Valley National Monument proposal, which includes nearly two million acres, is, in area, relatively modest among ten other pieces of Alaska that are similarly projected for confirmation by Congress as new parks and monuments. In all, these lands constitute over thirty-two million acres, which is more than all the Yosemites, all the Yellowstones, all the Grand Canyons and Sequoias put together—a total that would more than double the present size of the National Park System. For cartographic perspective, thirty-two million acres slightly exceeds the area of the state of New York.

Impressive as that may seem, it is less than a tenth of Alaska, which consists of three hundred and seventy-five million acres. From the Alaska Purchase, in 1867, to the Alaska Statehood Act, of 1958, Alaskan land was almost wholly federal. It was open to homesteading and other forms of private acquisition, but—all communities included—less than half of one percent actually passed to private hands. In the Statehood Act, the national government promised to transfer to state ownership a hundred and three million acres, or a little more than a quarter of Alaska. Such an area, size of California, was deemed sufficient for the needs of the population as it was then and as it might be throughout the guessable future. The generosity of this apportionment can be measured beside the fact that the 1958 population of Alaska—all natives included—was virtually the same as the population of Sacramento. Even now, after the influx of new people that followed statehood and has attended the building of the Trans-Alaska Pipeline and the supposed oil-based bonanza, there are fewer people in all Alaska than there are in San Jose. The central paradox of Alaska is that it is as small as it is large—an immense landscape with so few people in it that language is stretched to call it a frontier, let alone a state. There are four hundred thousand people in Alaska, roughly half of whom live in or around Anchorage. To the point picayunity, the state's road system is limited. A sense of the contemporary appearance of Alaska virtually requires inspection, because the civilized imagination cannot cover such quantities of wild land. Imagine, anyway, going from New York to Chicago—or, more accurately, from the one position to the other—in the year 1500. Such journeys, no less wild, are possible, and then some, over mountains, through forests, down the streams of Alaska. Alaska is a fifth as large as the contiguous forty-eight states. The question now is, what is to be the fate of all this land? It is anything but a "frozen waste." It is green nearly half the year. As never before, it has caught the attention of conflicting interests (developers, preservers, others), and events of the nineteen-seventies are accelerating the arrival of the answer to that question.

For a time, in the nineteen-sixties, the natives of Alaska succeeded in paralyzing the matter altogether. Eskimos, Indians, and Aleuts, in coordination, pressed a claim that had been largely ignored when the Statehood Act was passed. Observing while a hundred and three million acres were legislatively prepared for a change of ownership, watching as exploration geologists came in and found the treasure of Arabia under the Arctic tundra, the natives proffered the point that their immemorial occupancy gave them special claim to Alaskan land. They engaged attorneys. They found sympathy in the federal courts and at the highest levels of the Department of the Interior. The result was that the government offered handsome compensations. Alaska has only about sixty thousand natives. They settled for a billion dollars and forty million acres of land.

The legislation that accomplished this (and a great deal more) was the Alaska Native Claims Settlement Act, of 1971. Among events of significance in the history of Alaska, this one probably stands even higher than the Statehood Act and the treaty of purchase, for it not only changed forever the status and much of the structure of native societies; it opened the way to the Trans-Alaska Pipeline, which is only the first of many big-scale projects envisioned by development-minded Alaskans, and, like a jewel cutter's chisel cleaving a rough diamond, it effected the wholesale division, subdivision, patenting, parcelling, and deeding out of physiographic Alaska.

Because conservationists were outraged by the prospective pipeline, Congress attempted to restore a balance by including in the Native Claims Settlement Act extensive conservation provisions. The most notable of these was a paragraph that instructed the Secretary of the Interior to choose land of sufficient interest to its national owners, the people of the United States, to be worthy of preservation not only as national parks and national wild rivers but also as national wildlife refuges and national forests—some eighty million acres in all. Choices would be difficult, since a high proportion of Alaska could answer the purpose. In the Department of the Interior, an Alaska Planning Group was formed, and various agencies began proposing the lands, lakes, and rivers they would like to have, everywhere—from the Malaspina Glacier to Cape Krusenstern, from the Porcupine drainage to the Aniakchak Caldera.

Congress gave the agencies—gave the Secretary of the Interior— up to seven years to study and to present the case for each selection among these national-interest lands. Personnel began moving north. Pat Pourchot, for example, just out of college, had taken the Civil Service examination and then had wandered around the Denver Federal Center looking for work. He had nothing much in mind and was ready for almost any kind of job that might be offered. He happened into the Bureau of Outdoor Recreation. Before long, he was descending Alaskan rivers. He had almost no experience with canoes or kayaks or with backpacking or camping, but he learned swiftly. John Kauffmann (a friend of mine of many years) had been planning new Park System components, such as the C.&O. Canal National Historical Park and the Cape Cod National Seashore. Transferring to Alaska, he built a house in Anchorage, and soon cornered as his special province eight and a third million acres of the central Brooks Range. When confirmed by Congress, the area will become Gates of the Arctic National Park. It is a couple of hundred miles wide, and is east of the Salmon River.

For five years, he has walked it, flown it, canoed its rivers—camped in many weathers below its adze-like rising peaks. Before he came up here, he was much in the wild (he has been a ranger in various places and is the author of a book on eastern American rivers), but nonetheless he was a blue-blazer sort of man, who could blend into the tussocks at the Metropolitan Club. Unimaginable, looking at him now. If he were to take off his shirt and shake it, the dismembered corpses of vintage mosquitoes would fall to the ground. Tall and slim in the first place, he is now spare. After staring so long at the sharp, flinty peaks of the central Brooks Range, he has come to look much like them. His physiognomy, in sun and wind, has become, more or less, grizzly. Any bear that took a bite of John Kauffmann would be most unlikely to complete the meal.

Now, resting on a gravel island not far from the confluence of the Salmon and the Kobuk, he says he surely hopes Congress will not forget its promises about the national-interest lands. Some conservationists, remaining bitter about the pipeline, tend to see the park and refuge proposals as a sop written into the Native Claims Settlement Act to hush the noisome ecomorphs. Those who would develop the state for its economic worth got something they much wanted with their eight hundred miles of pipe. In return, the environmentalists were given a hundred and thirty words on paper. All the paragraph provided, however, was that eighty million acres could be temporarily set aside and studied. There was no guarantee of preservation to follow. The Wilderness Society, Friends of the Earth, the Sierra Club, the National Audubon Society, and other conservation organizations have formed the Alaska Coalition to remind Congress of its promise, of its moral obligation, lest the proposed park and refuge boundaries slowly fade from the map.

The temperature is in the low seventies. Lunch is spread out on the ground. We have our usual Sailor Boy Pilot Bread (heavy biscuits, baked in

Tacoma), peanut butter, jam, and a processed cheese that comes out of a tube—artifacts of the greater society, trekked above the Arctic Circle. Other, larger artifacts may be coming soon. The road that has been cut beside the Trans-Alaska Pipeline will eventually be open to the public. Then, for the first time in human history, it will be possible to drive a Winnebago—or, for that matter, a Fleetwood Cadillac—from Miami Beach to the Arctic Ocean. Inevitably, the new north road will develop branches. One projected branch will run westward from the pipeline to Kotzebue and Kivalina, on the Chukchi Sea. The road alignment, which Congress could deflect in the name of the national-interest lands, happens to cross the Salmon River right here, where we are having lunch. We are two hundred and fifty miles from the pipeline. We are three hundred and fifty miles from the nearest highway. Yet here in the tundra plain, and embedded in this transparent river, will stand perhaps, before long, the piers of a considerable bridge. I squeeze out the last of the cheese. It emerges from the tube like fluted icing.

There is little left of the river, and we cover it quickly—the canoe and the single kayak bobbing lightly, Snake Eyes riding low, its deck almost at water level. The meanders expand and the country begins to open. At the wide mouth of the Salmon, the gravel bottom is so shallow that we get out and drag Snake Eyes. We have come down through the mountains, and we have more recently been immured between incised stream banks in the lower plain, and now we walk out onto a wide pebble beach on the edge of a tremendous river. Gulfs of space reach to horizon mountains. We can now see, far to the northeast, the higher, more central Brooks Range, blurred and blue and soft brown under white compiled flat-bottomed clouds. There are mountains south of us, mountains, of course, behind us. The river, running two full miles to the nearest upstream bend, appears to be a lake. Mergansers are cruising it. The Kobuk is, in places, wide, like the Yukon, but its current is slower and has nothing of the Yukon's impelling, sucking rush. The Yukon, like any number of Alaskan rivers, is opaque with pulverized rock, glacial powder. In a canoe in such a river, you can hear the grains of mountains like sandpaper on the hull. Glaciers are where the precipitation is sufficient to feed them. Two hundred inches will fall in parts of southern Alaska, and that is where the big Alaskan glaciers are. Up here, annual precipitation can be as low as fifteen inches. Many deserts get more water from the sky. The Arctic ground conserves its precipitation, however—holds it frozen half the year. So this is not a desert. Bob Fedeler, whose work with Alaska Fish and Game has taken him to rivers in much of the state, is surprised by the appearance of the Kobuk. "It is amazing to see so much clear water," he says. "In a system as vast as this one, there is usually a glacial tributary or two, and that mucks up the river."

Standing on the shore, Fedeler snaps his wrist and sends a big enameled spoon lure, striped like a barber pole, flying over the water. Not long after it splashes, he becomes involved in a struggle with something more than a grayling. The fish sulks a little. For the most part, though, it moves. It makes runs upriver, downriver. It dashes suddenly in the direction of the tension on the line. His arms now oscillating, now steady, Fedeler keeps the line taut, keeps an equilibrium between himself and the fish, until eventually it flops on the dry gravel at his feet. It is a nine-pound salmon, the beginnings of dinner. Stell Newman catches another salmon, of about the same size. I catch one, a seven-pound adolescent, and let it go. Pat Pourchot, whose philosophical abstinence from fishing has until now been consistent, is suddenly aflush with temptation. Something like a hundred thousand salmon will come up the Kobuk in a summer. (They are counted by techniques of aerial survey.) The Kobuk is three hundred miles long and has at least fifty considerable tributaries—fifty branching streams to which salmon could be returning to spawn—and yet when they have come up the Kobuk to this point, to the mouth of the Salmon River, thirty thousand salmon turn left. As school after school arrives here, they pause, hover, reconnoitre—prepare for the run in the home stream. The riffles we see off-shore are not rapids but salmon. Pourchot can stand it no longer. He may have phased himself out of fishing, but he is about to phase himself back in. Atavistic instincts take him over. His noble resolve collapses in the presence of this surge of fish.

He borrows Fedeler's rod and sends the lure on its way. He reels. Nothing. He casts again. He reels. Nothing. Out in the river, there may be less water than salmon, but that is no guarantee that one will strike. Salmon do not feed on the spawning run. They apparently bite only by instinctive reflex if something flashes close by them. Pourchot casts again. Nothing. He casts again. The lure this time stops in the river as if it were encased in cement. Could be a boulder. Could be a submerged log. The lure seems irretrievably snagged—until the river erupts. Pourchot is a big man with a flowing red beard. He is well over six feet. Blond hair tumbles across his shoulders. The muscles in his arms are strong from many hundreds of miles of paddling. This salmon, nonetheless, is dragging him up the beach. The fish leaps into the air, thrashes at the river surface, and makes charging runs of such thrust that Pourchot has no choice but to follow or break the line. He follows—fifty, seventy-five yards down the river with the salmon. The fish now changes plan and goes upstream. Pourchot follows. The struggle lasts thirty minutes, and the energy drawn away is almost half Pourchot's. He wins, though, because he is bigger. The fish is scarcely larger than his leg. When, finally, it moves out of the water and onto the gravel, it has no hook in its mouth. It has been snagged, inadvertently, in the dorsal fin. Alaska law forbids keeping any sport fish caught in that way. The salmon must take the lure in its mouth. Pourchot extracts the hook, gently lifts the big fish in his arms, and walks into the river. He will hold the salmon right side up in the water until he is certain that its shock has passed and that it has regained its faculties. Otherwise, it might turn bottom up and drown.

If that were my fish, I would be inclined to keep it, but such a thought would never cross Pourchot's mind. Moreover, one can hardly borrow the rod of a representative of the Alaska Department of Fish and Game, snag a salmon while he watches, and stuff it in a bag. Fedeler, for his part, says he guesses that ninety-five percent of salmon caught that way are kept. Pourchot removes his hands. The salmon swims away.

Forest Eskimos, who live in five small villages on the Kobuk, do not tend to think in landscape terms that are large. They see a river not as an entity but as a pageant of parts, and every bend and eddy has a name. This place, for example—this junction of rivers—is Qalugruich paanga, which, tightly translated, means "salmon mouth." For thousands of years, to extents that have varied with cycles of plenty, the woodland Eskimos have fished here. The wall tent of an Eskimo fish camp—apparently, for the time being, empty—stands a mile or so downstream. We find .30—'06 cartridge cases sprinkled all over the beach, and a G.I. can opener of the type that comes with C rations. With the exception of some old stumps—of trees that were felled, we imagined, by a hunting party cutting firewood—we saw along the Salmon River no evidence whatever of the existence of the human race. Now we have crossed into the outermost band of civilization—suggested by a tent, some cartridge cases, by a can opener. In the five Kobuk River villages—Noorvik, Kiana, Ambler, Shungnak, and Kobuk—live an aggregate of scarcely a thousand people. Kiana, the nearest village to us, is forty miles downstream. In recent years, caribou and salmon have been plentiful nearer home, and the people of Kiana have not needed to come this far to fish, else we might have found the broad gravel beach here covered with drying racks—salmon, split and splayed, hanging from the drying racks—and people seining for the fish going by.

We get back into the boats, shove off, and begin the run down the Kobuk. Paddling on a big lake is much the same. You fix your eye on a point two miles away and watch it until it puts you to sleep. The river bottom, nearly as distinct as the Salmon's, is no less absorbing. It is gravelled, and lightly covered with silt. In shallow places, salmon leave trails in the silt, like lines made by fingers in dust. Eskimos know that one school of salmon will follow the trails of another. In shallow bends of the river, fishing camps are set up beside the trails. "We must have fish to live," the people say; and they use ever part of the salmon. They eat the eggs with bearberries. They roast, smoke, fry, boil, or dry the rest. They bury the heads in leaf-lined pits and leave them for weeks. The result is a delicacy reminiscent of cheese. Fevers and colds are sometimes treated by placing fermented salmon on the skin of the neck and nose. A family might use as many as a thousand salmon a year. To feed dogs, many salmon are needed. Dogs eat whole fish, and they clean up the fins, intestines, and bones of the fish eaten by people. Dog teams have largely been replaced by snowmobiles (or snow machines, as they are almost universally called in Alaska), and, as a result, the salmon harvest at first declined. Snow machines, however—for all their breathtaking ability to go as fast as fifty miles an hour over roadless terrain—break down now and again, and are thus perilous. A stranded traveller cannot eat a snow machine. Dog teams in the region are increasing in number, and the take of salmon is growing as well.

Now, for the first time in days of river travel, we hear the sound of an engine. A boat rounds a bend from the west and comes into view—a plywood skiff, two women and a man, no doubt on their way from Kiana to Ambler. A thirty-five-horsepower Evinrude shoves them upcurrent. They wave and go by. There are a few kayaks in the villages, small ones for use in stream and lake hunting, but the only kayaks we are at all likely to see are the one-man Klepper and Snake Eyes.

Four miles from Qualugruich paanga, it is five in the day and time to quit. We are, after all, officially an extension of bureaucracy. Walking far back from the water, Kauffmann picks tent sites on beds of sedge. A big cottonwood log, half buried in sand, will be a bench by the fire. Mosquitoes swarm. They are not particularly bad. In this part of Alaska, nearer the coast, they sometimes fly in dense, whirling vertical columns, dark as the trunks of trees. But we have not seen such concentrations. Kauffmann talks of killing forty at a slap in the Gates of the Arctic, but the season is late now and their numbers are low. I slap my arm and kill seven.

The temperature of the Kobuk is fifty-seven degrees—so contrastingly warm after the river in the mountains that we peel off our clothes and run into the water with soap. However, by no possible illusion is this the Limpopo, and we shout and yell at the cold water, take short, thrashing swims, and shiver in the bright evening sun. The Kobuk, after all, has about the same temperature—at this time of year—as the coastal waters of Maine, for which the term most often heard is "freezing." Wool feels good after the river; and the fire, high with driftwood, even better; and a dose of Arctic snakebite medicine even better than that. In a memo to all of us written many weeks ago, Pourchot listed, under "optional personal equipment," "Arctic snakebite medicine." There are no snakes in Alaska. But what if a snake should unexpectedly appear? The serum in my pack is from Lynchburg, Tennessee.

The salmon—filleted, rolled in flour, and sautéed on our pancake grill—is superb among fishes and fair among salmon. With few exceptions, the Pacific salmon that run in these Arctic rivers are of the variety known as chum. Their flesh lacks the high pink color of the silver, the sockeye, the king salmon. Given a choice among those, a person with a lure would not go for chum, and they are rarely fished for sport. After sockeyes and humpbacks, though, they are third in the commercial salmon fishery. Many millions of dollars' worth are packed each year. Athapaskan Indians, harvesting from the Yukon, put king salmon on their own tables and feed chum salmon to their dogs. Hence, they call chum "dog salmon." Eskimos up here in the Arctic Northwest, who rarely see another kind, are piqued when they hear this Indian term.

We look two hundred yards across the Kobuk to spruce that are reflected in the quiet surface. The expanded dimensions of our surroundings are still novel. Last night, in forest, we were close by the sound of rushing water. Sound now has become inverse to the space around us, for we sit in the middle of an immense and almost perfect stillness. We hear the fire and, from time to time, insects, birds. The sound of an airplane crosses the edge of hearing and goes out again. It is the first aircraft we have heard.

Kauffmann says he is worried, from the point of view of park planning, about the aircraft access that would probably be developed for the Salmon River. "It's not a big world up there. I'm not sure how much use it could take."

This reminds Fedeler of the cost of travel to wilderness, and makes him contemplate again who can pay to get there. "The Salmon is a nice enough river," he says. "But it is unavailable to ninety-nine point nine percent of the people. I wouldn't go back to Fairbanks and tell everybody they absolutely *have* to go and see the Salmon River."

"It's a fine experience."

"If you happen to have an extra six hundred bucks. Is the Park Service going to provide helicopter access or Super Cub access to some gravel bar near the headwaters?"

"Why does there have to be access?" Pourchot puts in.

"Why do there have to be wild and scenic rivers?" Fedeler wants to know. "And why this one—so far up here? Because of the cost of getting to it, the Salmon Wild River for most people would be just a thing on a map—an occasional trip for people from the Park Service, the Bureau of Outdoor Recreation, and the Alaska Department of Fish and Game. Meanwhile, with pressures what they are farther south, the sportsman in Alaska is in for some tough times."

"His numbers are increasing."

"And his opportunities are decreasing, while these federal proposals would set aside lands and rivers that only the rich can afford."

"The proposals, up here, are for the future," Kauffmann says, and he adds, after a moment, "As Yellowstone was. Throughout the history of this country, it's been possible to go to a place where no one has camped before, and now that kind of opportunity is running out. We must protect it, even if artificially. The day will come when people will want to visit such a wilderness—saving everything they have in order to see it, at whatever cost. We're talking fifty and more years hence, when there may be nowhere else to go to a place that is wild and unexplored."

I have a net over my head and cannot concentrate on this discussion, because something worse, and smaller, than mosquitoes—clouds of little flying prickers that cut you up—are in the air around us now and are coming through the mesh of the head net. They follow us into the tents, ignoring the netting there. They cut rashes into our faces all through the night.

V. SWANSON

Journal, 1917

OCT. 4TH, 1917. Getting sick packing, now looking for camping place.
   Cold in the lungs with a high fever.

6th. Less fever, less pain, but getting weak.

7th. Feeling better but very weak.

9th. Getting a little stronger.

10th. Going to build a house. Will not be able to pull canoe up this fall, got
   to wait for the ice.

13th. Shot a glacier bear.

14th. Shot a goat.

---

*This 1917 diary was discovered next to the body of an adventurer, found
dead in his cabin deep in the Alaskan wilderness. In 1939 it was reprinted
in the Federal Writers Project book on Alaska.*

17th. House finished.

18th. Taking out some traps.

20th. Made a smoke house.

21st. Shot one goat.

25th. Shot one lynx.

27th. Shot a wolf and a bear cub.

28th. Winter has come. Strong wind, two feet of snow.

Nov. 4th. Shot one lynx.

6th. Made one pair of bearskin pants.

8th. Sugar is all gone.

13th. Made two pair of moccasins.

18th. Finished one fur coat of bear, wolf, and lynx.

21st. Finished one sleeping bag of bear, goat, blankets, and canvas. Rain for several days.

22nd. Left eye bothers me. Shot one goat.

26th. Shot one lynx while eating breakfast.

27th. Made one pair of bearpaw snowshoes.

Dec. 1st. Getting bad. Cold for several days, river still open.

4th. River raised six feet in 24 hours.

6th. Slush stiffening, slowly making ice.

7th. The wind is so strong that you can't stand upright. River froze except a few riffles. Too much snow and too rough for sleighing. Snow getting deeper now.

15th. Very cold and strong wind, impossible to be out without skin clothes.

19th. Snowing but still very cold. Riffles up in the bend still open. Can't travel. Don't believe there will be ice a man can run a sleigh over this winter. Very little grub, snow too deep and soft for hunting goats. Stomach balking at straight meat, especially lynx.

21st. Shot a goat from the river.

25th. Very cold. A good Christmas dinner. Snow getting hard. River still open in places above camp.

26th. Broke through the ice. Skin clothes saved the day.

31st. Finished new roof on the house. One month of cold weather straight. Last night and today rain. Stomach getting worse.

Jan. 8th, 1918. River open as far as can be seen. Health very poor.

12th. Lynx moving down the river one or two a night; no chance to catch them.

15th. Goats moving out of reach. Using canoe on the river.

16th. One lynx. Weather getting mild.

20th. Rain today.

22nd. One lynx.

28th. One goat, been cold for a few days, no ice on river.

Feb. 1st. Cold weather nearly all month of January. Lynx robbed my meat cache up river. Salt and tea but once a day. Gradually getting weaker.

5th. Colder weather, feeling very bad. Just able to take care of myself.

10th. Milder, feeling very bad. Heavy fall of snow.

15th. Good weather continues, feeling some better.

24th. More snow. Living on dry meat and tallow.

26th. Shot one goat from the river.

Mch. 2nd. Shot one goat.

11th. Starting for Dry Bay, believing the river open. Out about one hour and struck ice. Can't go either way. Too weak to haul the canoe. Snow soft, no game here.

25th. Trying to get to the house. River is frozen in places and rising. The sleigh is now only three miles from there, but open river and perpendicular cliffs keep me from getting any farther. At present cannot find anything to eat here. Eyes are getting bad.

28th. Eyes can't stand the sun at all. Finest kind of weather.

Apr. 1st. Got to the house with what I could carry. Wolverines have been here eating my skins, robes, and moccasins, old meat, and also my goatskin door. They tried to run me last night, came through the stovepipe hole showing fight. Heavy fall of snow. Canoe and some traps down the river about five miles, close to Indian grave mark. Camp about halfway.

3rd. Still snowing. Cooking my last grub, no salt, no tea.

4th. Shot one goat, using all but three of my shells. Can't see the sights at all.

7th. Wolverine working on camp below carrying away my things. Ate part of my bearskin pants. Packed the old .30-.30 out into the brush. Eyes getting worse again, don't even stand the snow.

10th. Wolverines at my bedding and one snowshoe. In the tent, getting shaky in the legs. A five-mile walk a big day's work.

12th. Seen a fox track today. Birds are coming too. Fine weather.

15th. The no-salt diet is hitting me pretty hard. Eyes are getting worse, in the bunk most of the time.

17th. Rain yesterday and today.

20th. Finest weather continues again, cooking the last grub, got to stay in bunk most of the time—my legs won't carry me very far. My eyes are useless for hunting, the rest of my body also useless. I believe my time has come. My belongings, everything I got I give to Joseph Pellerine of Dry Bay; if not alive, to Paul Swartzkoph, Alsek River, April 22, 1918.

ALASTAIR SCOTT

Tracks Across Alaska

"AH-WAH-HAGH-OO-AR!" is actually an obsolete term which was last used in a different region a century ago. "MUSH!", the most celebrated command, may mean something to film directors but it means nothing to sled dogs. It is a corruption of "*marche!*" and was borrowed from French-Canadian dog-drivers, who used it as their starting shout. Archbishop Hudson Stuck was still shouting "MUSH!" at the turn of the century but it most have disappeared shortly after this, only to be revived as a name for the sport and its practitioners: mushing and mushers.

North American dog commands have been standardized because

A veteran traveler from the Scottish Highlands, Alastair Scott got the notion of dogsledding across Alaska while stewing up "a pot of simmering sheep's heads." After much training, Scott began across the Iditarod Trail —the route of the famous race. The result was recorded in Tracks Across Alaska *(1990).*

a common jargon makes exchanging dogs easier. There are variations but the basic commands are: ALL RIGHT or LET'S GO (to start,) HIKE or GET UP (faster), HAW (left), GEE (right), ON BY or STRAIGHT AHEAD, EASY (slow down), and WHOA (stop). Tone of voice is important: sharp, short, excited sounds to encourage action, and long, soothing ones to reduce the level of action. "WHOA!" yelled urgently can, as I discovered, produce the same effect as "HIKE!"

A sled has no form of steering. It is not particularly manoeuvrable but by adjusting one's weight, using the handlebars to lever a runner off the snow or, in desperation, jumping off and hauling the sled over while on the run, small changes of direction can be achieved and obstacles which the dogs side-step can be avoided. The more I learned, the more I realized how little I knew, and how much knowledge was needed.

I had no idea what, how much, or how often to feed a sled dog. I had little notion of how mushing worked, so could barely guess at the amounts and methods of training my dogs and I would need. I didn't even have any dogs yet and hadn't heard of any offer. My funds were running low. Furthermore, it was perfectly obvious that the route I had doodled around Alaska in three cheerful colors, which had failed to impress Schweppes, Rest Assured Beds, and thirteen others, was wildly ambitious. The logistics of organizing such a trip, or any trip, became too awful to contemplate. My ignorance weighed heavily enough without adding these.

One evening I sat down to approach the problems methodically, starting with the easiest. I would shorten my proposed journey from the original 2,500 miles to one of 800 miles, and my destination would be Nome. I had been reading about a diphtheria epidemic which struck this town in 1925, and about a relay of dog teams which rushed serum there. I now intended to follow their route. The next problem, the difficulty of learning how to handle and care for sled dogs, had no quick solution. It was a matter of application, and I could do no more than sink all my time and energy into being among dogs. Finding a team of my own remained my chief anxiety. I had come to Manley because of the offer of a cabin. Now it seemed that Manley's dogs were sprint racers, too light and thin-coated for my purposes.

Before leaving Scotland I had written to Alaskan newspapers asking if an enclosed request for information about dogs could be forwarded to local dog clubs or enthusiasts. I had received only one reply and this, remarkably, from one of the best-known distance-racers in North America. Susan Butcher had offered to help me, and she happened to live only twenty miles from Manley. I had not been able to contact her since my arrival, but I knew that her dogs were much in demand, and priced accordingly. Puppies and novices were out because I had neither the time nor the know-how to train dogs from scratch. I needed dogs who could teach me. To find a trained dog which was inexpensive *and* good was a matter of rare luck. Cheap dogs were usually problem dogs. My best hope lay in becoming the "caretaker" of a reasonable team for someone who wanted a season off from mushing.

The first two weeks of November were spent working with Joee and Pam. I started each day at the very bottom, as every dog owner starts each day, cleaning the "office." The daylight hours were used for running teams, the evenings were taken up with feeding, and the odd moments throughout were filled with clipping nails, trimming paw fur, pouring drinking water and playing the goat with all the staff. Mushing, however serious, must always include fun.

Little by little my understanding increased and brought ever deepening respect for these animals. We shared up to twelve hours a day together, and I never tired of their company. They won me over. I was completely hooked.

Then one day (it was 16 November) Joee shouted from the woods beyond his dog lot. "Come over here. I want to show you something."

He led me to three dogs I had not noticed before, the excess from the craterland. They were chained to trees and had trodden their own craters. The first was a female, as large as any of the other dogs in the lot, weighing about fifty pounds. Her coat was flecked with silver but she was predominantly golden with a black-tinted saddle and dark muzzle. Her broad head was beautifully proportioned. She looked alert and intelligent but her eyes expressed resignation, a sense of hopelessness.

"That's Silver. See how she likes you." He meant it as no test, for he knew Silver liked everyone. She sprang into a half-curvet, confidently expecting me to catch her front legs. She was gentle and licking and yet a wedge of caution remained, as if she read into me another of life's false promises.

"She's a leader, only six years old. She was never fast enough for my team so we used her as a puppy trainer. Then she got bored having to take out noisy pups twice a day round the same circuit, and at the end of the season having to run like hell to keep ahead of them. She just sat down on us and refused to go. We haven't run her since last season. She's sort of retired now."

The next dog was a cream-colored male of average size. Sensor had a pink blotch on his black nose and was nervously bouncy. He demonstrated three fast circuits of his domain, barked excitedly, and in an instant had disappeared into his house. He was not used to an audience.

The third dog was the strangest creature in sight. Alf was black except for a white muzzle, white chest, white socks, and a white tip to his tail. The others *looked* like sled dogs but Alf, part terrier, was simply a scruff. He had a droopy moustache. His long hair, exceptionally fine, was tousled and stuck out in a manner suggesting a state of permanent shock. (Except for the color, an acquaintance was to point out later, Alf and I at least had something in common.)

"He's a bit shy," Joee cautioned. A single glance at Alf and he slunk away to the extremity of his chain. He let me stroke him at arm's length, but it was an ordeal to be endured. He sat stiffly, looking at me through the corners of his eyes, his lower jaw pulled to one side in a grimace.

"Why is he so afraid?"

"He never got enough attention as a puppy." Joee explained that a critical period in a puppy's development occurs between its fourth and sixth weeks. It never forgets what it learns in this period. If it is played with and given lots of handling at this stage, it learns to trust people. If this is neglected, months or years of hard work may be needed to win its confidence. Alf had been raised by another breeder and given to Joee. "Alf and Sensor are only two-year-olds but they aren't shaping up for my purposes. Why don't you borrow these dogs and maybe I can dig out an old sled for you. That way you can at least goof around here, see what it's all about and make the mistakes we all have to make."

His generosity did not stop there. Joee lent me doghouses, harnesses, bowls and enough food to tide me over until I could arrange transport to Fairbanks to buy my own supplies. I sited the doghouses among trees close to my cabin and cleared an access trail. That evening, with a sled parked outside my cabin door, a bucket of warm feed to hand and six neon-bright eyes catching the light of my headlamp, I felt I had arrived. I believed I was almost halfway to Nome.

Optimism's stultifying effect on our perception is its major virtue. In reality my problems were only beginning.

OPTIMISM AND LUCK abounded in this hard country, though, as in the story of Fairbanks' founding. In 1901 Captain E. T. Barnette hired the skipper of the flat-bottomed *Isabelle* to ferry a cargo of supplies up the

Tanana River into little-known territory. Captain Barnette had been a placer miner in Washington. He had no boat of his own and knew nothing about boats, for he had adopted the rank of captain during a five-year jail sentence for stealing his partner's share of gold. His intention was to build a trading post at what is now Tanacross, to intercept the traffic of miners between Valdez and the Klondike where their route crossed the Tanana River. He had promised an acquaintance to name the post for Senator Fairbanks of Indiana.

Laden with the post's considerable inventory the *Isabelle* was unable to negotiate shallows far downstream from Barnette's goal. In an effort to get round the obstruction, the skipper entered Chena Slough, proceeded a few miles and hit bottom once again. Notwithstanding that he was still 175 miles from his potential clients and in an area containing only a handful of prospectors, Barnette refused to turn back. He unloaded his outfit onto the bank. The *Isabelle* steamed off downstream to escape the approach of winter, leaving two figures alone in the wilderness. Beside the tall heap of his belongings Barnette watched the boat go. His wife sobbed on his shoulder. The following summer a prospector called Felix Pedro made a rich strike a few miles away, and the Barnettes could not have been better placed for Alaska's penultimate gold rush.

The pickings were difficult, however, and Fairbanks was slow to develop, but it was to prove the richest goldfield in Alaska. Within nine years the town had five churches, two hospitals, and twenty-three saloons. Ladies left visiting cards, with their preferred day for receiving visitors printed in a lower corner, on trays provided for the purpose by cabin doors. By 1912 Captain Barnette had made a fortune, started a bank, embezzled its money—it took Fairbanks three years to recover—been in and out of jail, and left in a state of personal ruin. Fairbanks might have fizzled out with the decreasing revenues from the mines, had it not been for its importance as a military base in the Second World War and as a construction center for the pipeline.

Today Fairbanks is a city of 50,000 people. It looks as though the number of churches and hospitals has stayed the same, and the saloons trebled. Its central grid of streets might belong to any city and crossing it is just as testing, for Fairbanks has more cars per head than Los Angeles. Yet no other downtown offers the chance of watching a dog team bowl past rush-hour traffic. The city straggles over a large area to include a university, a military base, industrial estates, satellite suburbs, and car parks equipped with electric sockets so engines can be plugged in and kept warm during winter. Fairbanks is a major trading post for the Interior. Its sales of alcohol, like those of Anchorage, are phenomenal. Inhabitants of dry villages across the north flock to it like pilgrims. It suited my interests admirably: easy to enter, easy to leave, well stocked with mushers' needs.

Passing through Fairbanks on my way to Manley several weeks earlier, I had gone to one of the state's largest banks and enquired about the fastest means of having money sent out from Scotland. It was best to arrange for a bank draft, I was told, to be sent by post. The clerk wrote down the bank's address, incorrectly. As a consequence, my first draft was returned to Scotland stamped "Address unknown," my funds disappeared for two months, I fell into debt to Manley, and eventually traveled a total of 1,300 miles in efforts to claim my money.

However, the full drama was yet to play itself out. This was only the second of four visits to Fairbanks. Another Manley musher, Eric Meffley, had given me a lift in his empty dog truck. I phoned the bank on arrival and was delighted to hear two drafts had arrived. They would be ready for collection that afternoon. During the morning I used the last of my travelers' checks to purchase enough supplies for my immediate needs.

Our last call was at a dog-feed company and on a notice-board there the following message was posted:

> SLED DOGS FOR SALE. Six dogs including two leaders, $900.
> R. Roberts, North Pole. Tel. —.

"Eric, could we . . . ?"

North Pole was twelve miles away. We drove there at once. R.
Roberts was about to become a father for the second time and needed the
money to pay maternity bills. Having only a novice's sentimentality to go
on, I asked Eric to examine the dogs and assess their worth. We decided on
four: Rosco, a black Siberian leader with white muzzle and clownish eyebrows; his sons, all-white Sisco, and Nanook, grey with a handsome mask;
and Kavik, a tough wheel dog whose white woolly coat was patched with
what appeared to be coyote. All were males; I wanted, as far as possible, to
avoid a mixed team and the complications of females coming into season.
We settle on a price of $650, to be paid when I returned later that after-
noon with the money. I hadn't suspected that the bank would arrange my
appointment for an afternoon on which they were closed; and, the following day, I could never have anticipated Bob Cranhoff.

Bob Cranhoff was a lanky streak of misery. Gaunt and balding,
he did not directly state that it was the likes of myself who had caused his
baldness, but his manner made it clear that at the very least I was ruining
his day.

"What *appears* to be the problem?" Bob Cranhoff, the manager,
asked. His words sounded on their last legs.

I handed him my two drafts, totalling $2,000, which had just been
passed along a line of his tellers and rejected.

"Ahh, bank drafts. I really can't understand why you don't have
your money cabled. Only takes twenty-four hours."

I explained that one of his staff had advised bank drafts *and* she had got the bank's address wrong.

He ignored this. "The problem now is that these drafts can only be drawn on, respectively, a bank in Los Angeles and a bank in New York. They will take at least two weeks to clear."

I told him about my journey and about the dogs. I explained that I only needed $650. It was a unique chance to buy these dogs. I was living 160 miles away without any means of transport. By next week the dogs might be sold, and after today I would no longer have the means of transporting them back to Manley. "Will you give me an advance on my drafts?"

He was shaking his head. "I admit it's ninety-nine percent certain that the banks will pay up, but I am not at liberty to give advances where there is *any* chance of risk. You are, in effect, asking for a loan."

"Then will you give me a loan? Maybe the dog-seller will accept a deposit at this state. Please—will you lend me something? Just two hundred dollars?"

He refused. My collateral was unacceptable. He excused himself and said he had already given me more of his time than he could spare. I presented my plea once more but he suddenly interrupted and stood up. Bob Cranhoff tensed and flushed. His forehead was puckered, his shoulders hunched. He held out his arms at quarter-mast and said in a thin, high-pitched voice: "Why . . . why did you choose my bank?"

I PHONED R. Roberts to apologize and let him know my funds had not come through. The deal was off. I returned despondently to Eric's truck with $1.60 in my pockets. Eric listened to my story and shrugged. "Don't worry. There'll be plenty more opportunities. You'll see." He stared at me for a moment, then took out his wallet and checked the contents.

"C'mon," he said, "let's go and get those dogs.'

SILVER, SENSOR, ALF, Rosco, Nanook, Sisco and Kavik. My new family.

Joee then added Duran, a powerful male with wolf markings and a superb physique. Of all "my" dogs, Duran would always catch the attention of experienced mushers first. Eric lent me two of his dogs who needed more attention than he could spare, and so from having no dogs I suddenly found myself with ten. I ran them in two teams and longed for the day when my expertise would enable me to take them out as one. My education suddenly began in earnest. I had first to get to know the personalities and temperaments of my dogs, and learn to read their body language. Each had its peculiarities. The gait, the angle of the ears, the level of the tail, the height of the head: these varied to suit an individual's style and any break in habit signified an unhappy dog. Dogs are like people. They have good days and off days. They can get bored, lazy, and mischievous. They catch bugs, go off their food, pull muscles, and fall in love.

I began keeping a record of my doings and observations. Each evening I would take several dogs into the cabin for a few hours so we could get to know each other more quickly. I would repair harnesses, make up ganglines, read books on sledding, and make entries in my log-book.

Some extracts from the dog log.

You don't get much sleep with dogs. Every day brings new anxieties and old ones linger on. Sensor has diarrhoea, but is eating. Duran's a bit dehydrated. A simple test. Pull up a handful of fur and skin above the shoulders and let go. If the skin instantly snaps back, all is well. If it slowly returns or stays up in a crease, the dog's dehydrated. The longer it takes the more serious it is. Two percent dehydration reduces performance by twenty percent. Dogs lose most fluid in *warm* and *very cold* conditions, and a dehydrated dog often refuses to drink. You have to dribble fluid into the back of its mouth (along its cheek) with a syringe. Joee says dehydration is the biggest problem on my trip. Sled dogs won't drink pure water—it needs to be flavored. They'll snap up snow while running but this is not enough. Each dog may need as much as a gallon of water a day.

Minus 30°F today. Can't use bowls for feeding as dogs' tongues will freeze to the metal. They eat their food off the snow. Every evening I spend 20 minutes rubbing ointment into dogs' feet as they lie in their houses. Have to do it in bursts as cold on the hands, though their toes are lovely and warm.

Silver can do everything expected of a leader but she's crafty. She has perfected the art of keeping a taut tugline without actually contributing to the movement of the sled. I tread a delicate line between being friendly and being taken advantage of. Leaders can be forgiven for not consistently pulling hard, but is she losing interest in the whole business? I need to know before we end up in a blizzard.

Now I've raved about every dog and had doubts about every dog. Sensor always lopes. The rest will be trotting along but he always lopes. Alf was useless—didn't pull, kept on tangling. Nanook got easily distracted and gave up. Yesterday he was the best of the lot. Duran only runs well on the left. Kavik is a grafter but I'm worried he has an aggressive side to him. I feel he's spoiling for a fight.

Rosco stops dead when I shout "whoa" and the swing dogs run into him. Must remember to brake first, shout second. Silver needs it the other way round!

Problems, problems—all with Rosco. He suddenly began ignoring "haw." Refused to acknowledge the possibility of left turns. Five times I had to stop and haul him round to the left. Is it the way I say it? Is he just stubborn?

They say you aren't a real musher unless you've repaired a chewed harness and lost your team. Today I became a real musher. During one run I dropped a mitten. Stopped to retrieve it. Stamped the snowhook into the trail and walked back. The next moment the dogs had taken off, ripping out the hook. "Whoa" had no effect. What a terrifying feeling, seeing your dogs and sled heading off into the distance. As a last hope I yelled "haw," anything to try and stop them. Silver turned "gee." perhaps it was easier for her. What a dog! She led them into deep snow and they stopped. I was lucky. Must *always* secure my sled before leaving it. My life may depend on it. Also, a loose team invariably ends up tangled, and then fights may break out. Dogs have often been injured or killed this way.

I've had enough of Alf. He just messes around. He chewed through two necklines today and ate a glove. Has the worst feet of all, so hairy they always gather iceballs. I'm forever having to stop to remove them. Leave them too long and they'll rub the skin raw between his toes. He also has web splits, as do several others. Am told their feet will toughen as the season progresses. So now have to use bootees on the bad feet—a big hassle but the only solution. Alf is as shy as ever—all my hours spent with him have done nothing. A waste of time. Am going to return him to Joee.

The Rosco saga continues. It *is* stubbornness. He only accepts left turns when he knows they are shortcuts to home. He'll never knowingly take a longer "left" route. (Why then does he accept a longer "right" route?) He's fine in areas he doesn't know—this gives me hope. But today he pulled Silver away from a correct turn. On Joee's advice I fell on him, held his muzzle and bit his ear (very sensitive). Hated doing it. He didn't like it either, but immediately refused the next left. I took him out of lead and put him in wheel. Meant to be degrading for a lead dog but unfortunately he seemed to like it. He's as stubborn as hell and yet I'm so fond of him. In the cabin he never leaves my side. Can I find a "right-turns-only" route to Nome?!

I think I've got it. I think Rosco *only* likes leading on his own. He's not totally cured, but what an improvement. I just tried it as an experiment, and he couldn't wag his tail hard enough. Funny business, this. Often it's not the dogs who are the slow learners.

I'm not going to hand Alf back. Can't do it. Though he's always been the renegade, I'm determined to win him over. I want to hand him back as a *real* sled dog. That's in the spirit of this whole thing. It wouldn't be right to walk into a ready-made team. Yet I can't afford to let the emotional side sway me. It's a question of finding dogs who won't give up when the going turns nasty. Things don't look too good at the moment; half the team in bootees, Rosco unreliable, Alf devouring my equipment, Sensor not drinking, Duran not eating, Sisco with soft stools. I wonder how much snow machines cost!?

IN ORDER TO try to understand Rosco's behavior I hunted out all the available literature on Siberian huskies. I didn't come across a great deal, and that little was of no help.

"The master of a sled team is revered by the Siberian Husky, who is by nature a loyal, affectionate dog. The commands of the master are followed eagerly by the team while out on the trail."

One book devoted pages to telling me how to give my husky a bath, which only made me envious. Another was obviously aimed at those who wanted the basics: a fantasy and a relaxing pre-dinner mush across the deep-pile carpet.

"The dog will wait expectantly each evening for the master's return from work, and will be overjoyed when he hears the jingle of keys at the door."

I threw the book away. My attention turned to the Iditarod. And it was about this time that I met Susan Butcher.

"THE LAST GREAT RACE ON EARTH"—A race over 1,049 miles of the roughest, most beautiful terrain Mother Nature has to offer. She throws jagged mountain ranges, frozen rivers, dense forests, desolate tundra, and miles of

windswept coast at the mushers and their dog teams. Add to that the temperatures far below freezing, winds that can cause complete loss of visibility, the
hazards of overflow, long hours of darkness and treacherous climbs and side
hills, and you have the IDITAROD.

EACH YEAR THE Iditarod brings a rush of excitement and media hype.
And though the writer of the official press release above has Mother
Nature throwing frozen rivers around as daunting obstacles (he clearly
hasn't visualized how many mushers and dogs would be lost if the rivers
weren't frozen), the essentials of his description stand. It is the longest sled
dog race in existence and there is nothing quite like it.

The Anchorage authorities spend most of the winter either grate-
ful for not having any snow or laying out considerable sums on getting rid
of the stuff, but come Iditarod time, they pay handsomely to have truck-
loads of snow hauled in and spread about the streets. The race starts in
downtown Anchorage on the first Saturday of March and ends in Nome
eleven days, two hours, five minutes and six seconds later, if the best-ever
time is equaled. The race stopwatch is activated as each musher leaves the
line on Fourth Avenue, but it stops twenty miles later at Eagle River. The
racers then climb into vehicles and transport their outfits thirty-five miles
to Settlers Bay where the real snowlands begin. A second staggered start
takes place here, the stopwatch continues where it left off, and the race
proper is under way. Time adjustments are made later at a compulsory rest
stop so that no advantage accrues from the starting order. After this, it is
the first to reach Nome who wins.

The route has a choice of two loops in its middle section, each being
used in alternate years. The northern loop, considered slightly tougher, passes
through Ruby, and the southern route goes via the ghost town of Iditarod.
The route is flagged along its length and a convoy of snow machines breaks

trail days ahead of the leaders, but neither measure is a guarantee against poor visibility or sudden dumps of snow. (Twenty inches have been known to fall in as many hours.) The total distance covered by either route is close to 1,150 miles, though the symbolic figure of 1,049 miles is more commonly touted. One hundred miles here or there don't mean much to promoters; much more sponsor-friendly is the fact that the race extends over approximately one thousand miles and takes place in the forty-ninth state.

There are twenty-two checkpoints between Anchorage and Nome, on average sixty miles apart. Automatic disqualification results if any item of mandatory equipment—axe, sleeping bag, snowshoes—is missing on arrival at a checkpoint. Weeks before the race mushers must send out sacks of food and supplies for distribution along the route and these may only be collected at checkpoints. The average racer will require 2,500 pounds of dog food and at least 1,000 bootees for the race. Most checkpoints are in villages where hospitality is available, a few are just crude shelters, but each has a vet who casts an eye over the dogs, offers free advice, medicines, vitamin injections, and can, if necessary, order a dog to be retired.

The rules of the Iditarod have been formulated largely to promote the welfare of the dogs. No team may contain more than eighteen. Each dog receives an identifying splotch of dye before leaving the starting line, and thereafter no dog may be substituted. Unfit dogs may be dropped off only at checkpoints, and are flown back to Anchorage. Teams are forced to withdraw if the number of active dogs in harness falls below five. Racers must take a twenty-four-hour rest sometime during the race at a checkpoint of their choice, and a compulsory six-hour layover at the last checkpoint, White Mountain, before the seventy-seven-mile dash for home.

Racers take part for fun, fame, and the usual "Everest" sort of reasons, but few hold expectations of making money. The first three or four finishers can expect to profit, largely through the indirect revenues of success—sponsorship, advertising, increased demand for their dogs—rather than the actual prize money. The purse varies from year to year according to the level of sponsorship but is generally around $250,000. This is shared out proportionately among the first twenty finishers, with the winner taking $30,000—50,000. If this seems extravagant, the costs of taking part are equally so. The entry fee is $1,249. The budget—conscious entrant will have little change from $11,000 by the time he or she has trained a team for the season, purchased equipment and food, trucked the dogs to Anchorage, flown them back from Nome and trucked them back again. To run the race on the scale of those who have a chance of winning can easily cost $25,000.

The Iditarod is one of two ultra-distance dog races, the other being the Yukon Quest which is several hundred miles shorter but with fewer checkpoints and considerably greater distance between them. It runs between Whitehorse in Canada's Yukon Territory and Fairbanks, the direction changing each year. Critics of the Iditarod assert that it has moved away from the spirit and tradition of the sport. It is theoretically possible for an Iditarod musher to complete the race in a series of sprints, sleeping each night under a roof and carrying no more than a light load of about a hundred pounds. The Quest, first run in 1984, was designed to test self-sufficiency and outdoorsmanship as much as dog driving ability. Competitors are restricted to smaller teams and, because of the distances between certain checkpoints, are obliged to camp out and carry loads of around 300 pounds. The Iditarod is long-distance Formula One, but the Quest is long-distance Rally. Both are grueling races but it is the Iditarod, the brainchild of Joe Redington, sen., which steals the limelight. Iditarod's gold rush, which had lured F. G. Manley to new heights of fortune at the cost of his hotel, peaked between 1910 and 1912 and was Alaska's last major stampede. During this period a trail was cut from the port of Seward to the mining camps of Iditarod, and then on to the Yukon River where it connected with the existing trail to Nome. By the time Old Joe, Joee's father, came to Alaska in 1948 and homesteaded near Knik on the old trail to Iditarod, the trail had fallen into disuse and grown over.

Joe Redington owned a husky within ten minutes of his arrival in Alaska and his live became centered on these animals. He was saddened to see the decline of sled dogs over the years and felt a marathon dog race, something sensational, might revive interest in them, especially if the purse were rich enough. In 1967, when Joe and some supporters first put forward the idea of reopening the Iditarod Trail and racing the length of it, the proposal was ridiculed. Then in 1972 the U.S. Army agreed to clear and mark the trail, and the project finally became feasible. The first race was held the following year and attracted twenty-two teams. Since then it has, even through sporadic bouts of insolvency, remained an annual event, and achieved everything Joe had hoped. A record field of seventy-six mushers and over a thousand dogs took part in 1986. Other sports have found inspiration in the event and a racing lexicon has been born: Iditaski, Iditaskate, Iditashoe . . .

In 1985 Libby Riddles became the first woman to win. Within a week sweatshirts were proclaiming "ALASKA—where men are men and women win the Iditarod." When another woman won it the following year, the theme stayed the same. "THE IDITAROD—where men hitch sleds to dogs and chase women across Alaska." When the same woman won it again, men grudgingly had to give more ground but they didn't give it all. "ALASKA—land of beautiful dogs and fast women."

The back-to-back winner was Susan Butcher. Each win had produced a new record time. This year she was going for a hat trick.

"WELL? WHAT YOU think?" Susan asked as I came in.

She didn't care for telephones. Her cabin at Eureka had only an emergency phone whose battery drained quickly. She and her husband, David Monson, usually stayed at Eureka to look after their kennel but once a week they took it in turn to have a day off. The day off was for a chore. Feeding, exercising, and cleaning up after their 250 dogs, six days a week, were the good things in life; talking on the phone was the chore. The Redingtons had a phone and so Susan and David traveled twenty miles to visit their friends and use it.

I had met Susan a week earlier when she was fully dressed. I had thought she was on the plump side but now it was apparent that I had been fooled by Yetification—the transformation through clothes and snow machine suits of any person into something large and lumbering. It happens to everyone in cold climates. She came as a jolt to my system, tired and damp as I was after a day's acrobatics behind a sled. It was hard to know what to think.

"To be honest," I replied, "the tie doesn't match, and I think the wind will get in the gaps. Is this your new Iditarod outfit?"

She stood before me wearing a bra, white boxer shorts patterned with an army of green frogs, a red necktie, a peaked cap with fixed head-lamp, and a pig's head around each foot. Their mouths gagged on Susan, their eyes looked up at the frogs, and it took a moment for me to fight down a feeling of revulsion and realize they were only pink fluff. Converted to statistics Susan Butcher was thirty-three, five feet six inches, just under ten stone, and had a body temperature, she affirmed, of 96.6°F—that is, two degrees lower than normal. She was extremely pretty. Her straight black hair, one-and-a-half dogs' tails long, fell down her back as a single braid. Her eyes were a very pale blue and vital, but it was her smile which really enhanced her features. Framed, it would have found a place on the wall of any dental surgery. Susan was loud and bubbling, and if she had sufficient natural padding against the cold, one could imagine it being the minimum required of a champion musher. Delighted with my vacant expression, she chuckled noisily and left the room without enlightening me.

"Christmas presents for David," explained Pam. "They've just arrived by mail order. She couldn't resist trying them on."

"The bra was her own," Joee added, unnecessarily.

Susan's world is dogs. Her favorites receive wrapped presents at Christmas. All are legally retained outside the terms of common ownership that marriage confers. Just as dogs often display two personalities—one in the doghouse, a very different one in harness—Susan's personality changes behind a sled. Her vision narrows to the trail width, the tomfoolery vanishes, she turns serious and will herself into her dogs. In an interview she once tried to explain this to the inhabitants of Manhattan. "You have to understand, this is all I care about, and this is all I think about. I'm with the dogs twelve hours a day. They're my friends and my family and my livelihood."

Eureka is a gold mining area worked by barely a shovelful of other residents. Forested hills and a river-filled gulch surround Susan's Trailbreaker Kennels. The center is a "village" of dog houses of which two are converted barrel stoves, Granite's still complete with smoke stack. He lies inside with his nose and front paws protruding through the fire door, as if in charge of Stevenson's Rocket. The largest wooden building is devoted to dog care and the others are single-roomed log cabins. The one used by David and Susan as a kitchen and office is the darkest. The previous owner had found the interior so blackened by decades of smoke he had dismantled the cable, swiveled each log about and rebuilt it inside-out.

One day I visited them at this cabin. David sat at a desk in one corner. A former South Dakotan, attorney, dog food salesman and Iditarod racer, he was always good-humored and ready to parry and thrust with his sharp wit. His trimmed beard and gold-rimmed spectacles gave him an academic look as he scribbled notes in preparation for the Yukon Quest (two months later, he won its $20,000 first prize with Trailbreaker's second-best team). Beside him Meaty the cat lay Swiss-rolled on top of a carpeted cat tower. A sick dog lay on the sofa while Susan yelled his symptoms into a microphone and a boxful of crackles. Above her, a sturdy shelf supported a complete set of *Encyclopedia Britannica.* Opposite and far from conspicuous on another shelf stood a pair of tall silver cups. Both were engraved "The Last Great Race." One held a pot plant.

Born in a place she never liked and raised in an unsettled family, Susan looked back on her childhood in Cambridge, Massachusetts, with little fondness except for two loves which developed during this period: of the outdoors, and of animals. She left home at the age of fifteen and was lured to Colorado by the go-west catchphrase. Here she discovered dog-sledding, the ideal combination of her loves. She worked with dog mushers and as a veterinary technician for four years, all the while realizing the west was no better than the east. "I came to Alaska for the same reason as David, though we hadn't met then. To find a place where you are judged by your performance, not your pedigree."

For two years she lived in a remote cabin in the Wrangell Mountains, doing nothing but mushing. Her tutor was Tekla, her first leader. Susan recalled an incident: crossing a frozen river, Tekla refused to "haw" and led the team away to the right. Seconds later, with a sharp report, the section of ice Susan had tried to cross caved in and was sucked under. She and the team were left on the edge, two sled-lengths from open water. This, the cold, the blizzards, and the Big Lonesome "were the times when I learnt Mother Nature was bigger than me."

The Iditarod was her goal right from the start. She developed a strong friendship with Joe Redington, sen., and he helped put together her first Iditarod team in 1978; in a joint venture the following year the two became the first to drive a dog team to the 20,320-foot summit of Denali

(Mount McKinley). She was placed nineteenth in her first race. By 1984 she had finished twice in ninth place, twice in fifth place, and twice in second. Always just ahead of her was a man called Rick Swenson.

On the first night of the 1985 race Susan found her way blocked by a pregnant moose which charged, ran into the middle of her team and struck out in a frenzy of kicking and stomping. Twice Susan tried to frighten it away with her parka and an axe but was forced to retreat. She had no gun and could only watch helplessly as her prize dogs, still clipped to their lines, were knocked down and trampled. By the time another racer came along and killed the moose with four shots of a .44 revolver, one dog was dead, one was fatally injured, and fifteen had injuries, from which they eventually recovered. Susan scratched from the race and watched an honor she coveted fall to someone else. That year the first to pass through the wooden arch in Nome was Libby Riddles.

The following year, in her ninth race, Susan at last saw her leaders, Granite and Mattie, presented with the garlands of victory—matching strings of plastic yellow roses (real ones would wild too quickly in the cold). With her second win in 1987, Susan confirmed her celebrity status. The chores of telephoning increased. Fan letters arrived at a rate of one hundred a month and a secretary had to be employed to answer them. They came addressed as vaguely as "Susan Butcher, Alaska" and "Granite, Iditarod"; and they were delivered. Now she was winning every race she entered and was the measure of every musher.

"Will you tell me your secret?" I asked.

"Sure," she replied. Her grin was almost as big as the banana *flambé* she was now cooking. "I've always had a way with animals. It was birth-given. I know the power of a dog's mind and can harness that power. I know how to shape a dog's attitude. I take my dogs running and swimming with me in summer. They come into the cabin, we play a lot, we have fun and I reckon we've developed a special bond. All my dogs love to race." She went on to explain that she had always made a dog's welfare and fitness her main concern and over the years this policy was showing its rewards. She had a good eye for a dog, bred them wisely, and culled those with bad feet, thin coats, and low stamina. Some of her dogs were seventh-generation Iditarod runners. She had thirty-one command leaders. Of her likely Iditarod team for that year, fourteen out of eighteen would be command leaders. An average musher would have felt blessed with four.

"You asked for my secret," she added "but it won't bring instant success. More *flambé*?"

The papers and sweatshirts had made much of Libby Riddles' and Susan Butcher's wins. Susan was irritated by the gender preoccupation. She saw no distinction between a female and a male dog driver. Her goal was simply to be the best in her chosen field: the world's best distance musher, the world's best dog person. The one who stood in her way was Rick Swenson.

No one had pulled in more Iditarod prize money than Rick Swenson. He had won the race four times and, until Susan's 1987 win, that was three times more than any other victor. Rick was acclaimed as the master tactician. In addition to breeding and training top dogs, he raced them with skill and employed the full arsenal of psychological warfare. Those who knew him well said he could be either the perfect charmer or, euphemistically, "real mean." He had lived in Eureka before Susan moved there, and they had become friends as well as neighbors.

Recently the friendship had soured. Rick left Eureka and moved his entire kennel close to Fairbanks, supposedly because the area's trails were better for training, but it was rumored he could no longer bear to be in Susan's shadow. His last win had been in 1982. Gossip columns lengthened on the affair. "To say there is bad blood between these two mushers is an understatement. A river of red runs here," wrote one monger. Earlier in his racing career Rick was variously referred to as the Mohammed Ali or the John McEnroe of dog sledding. When he failed to win he was lampooned, even though he seldom slipped lower than second or third place. His abusive comments were seized by the media and further demeaned his image. Some comments were inexcusable, others were simply ill-considered, made under duress: thoughts uttered under harassment by reporters, after days without sleep, and when a year's income was about to be halved, quartered, or lost.

It was hard to know the extent to which the animosity was genuine or just kept hot by the press. It was not a question I cared to put to Susan, or an issue I was particularly interested in—except for one strange fact. In 1985, the year of the moose, Susan Butcher married David Monson. The wedding was unusual. The ring-bearers were Tekla and Granite. The best man was a woman, and one of the bridesmaids was Rick Swenson.

As this year's Iditarod drew closer, the media eagerly awaited the red river with sharpened pencils. I took no part in the dispute. Susan and David befriended me and my cause. Invigorated by their enthusiasm (and too much *flambéed* brandy) I visualized myself passing under Nome's burly arch, and Silver and Rosco in hooplas of plastic roses.

That night I mushed my ten dogs under moonlight, and almost believed it possible.

ANNE MORROW LINDBERGH

The King Islanders

ESKIMO SPORTS
Tomorrow Afternoon at 4 P.M.
At Barracks Sq. and Water Front
ESKIMO "WOLF DANCE" IN COSTUME
At Arctic Brotherhood Hall 8 P.M.
Public Invited
LINDBERGHS' BE GUESTS OF HONOR

THE NUGGET, NOME'S daily telegraph bulletin, lay on the table, its
front page announcing the day's entertainment. We had arrived in this old

---

Anne Morrow Lindbergh was the author of several books, including Steep
Ascent, Listen to the Wind, *and* The Waves of the Future. *A pilot herself,
Lindbergh accompanied her husband, Charles, on many transcontinental
flights. "The King Islanders" is from her 1935 book,* North to the Orient.

Alaskan mining town after a short flight from Shishmaref Inlet. The night mists had melted when we woke the morning after our adventure with the duck hunters. In front of us glistened a promised land. This was the Alaska we had read of. Snow-capped mountains climbed ahead of us instead of flat wastes. Green valleys cut the morning light. And the sea, the Bering Sea, rising in the gap between two hills as we approached, burned brilliant blue. We followed the beach, a gleaming white line, toward Safety Harbor. A second white line ran parallel to the shore, like foam or scattered flowers. As we came nearer I saw it to be a tangled trail of driftwood, polished white by the surf after its long journey down the Yukon River, out into the Norton Sound, and up the coast to Nome. Pounding, dancing, tossing, all the way they had come, these white arms, these branches from an alien forest, to flower on a bare coast that had never known a tree. They were as startling to see here as the waxen stems of Indian pipe in the heart of green woods, ghostly visitors from another world.

No trees yet. We had come far south from Barrow, but there were still no trees on these green hills falling to the water's edge. A broad trail cut its way over the slope, rippling up and down, like a whip cracking in the air. An Eskimo trail, I supposed, until I saw a black beetle crawl around the corner. A car! A road! We had not seen a road for so long that I hardly recognized one.

A little later we were bumping along the same road on our way into town. It had been a trail in the Gold Rush days. Old roadhouses were stationed along the side, a day's dog-team journey apart over winter snow; we had already passed the second one in forty minutes. Dilapidated shingled buildings they were, fast becoming useless; for the airplane on skis is replacing the dog team. It is cheaper per pound to fly.

Nome has changed since the Gold Rush days when in the 1890s the precious metal was discovered in creeks and on the coast, and the great trail of prospectors swarmed over the mountains to that far cape of Alaska; when all the beach for miles—that white line we had seen from the air— was black with men sifting gold from the sand; when banks, hotels, the-aters, and shops sprang up overnight and busy crowds thronged up and down the plank streets. Twenty thousand people once filled the town; now there are hardly more than a thousand.

But there were still signs of the old life. We passed a deserted min-ing shack by a stream. Fireweed, yarrow, and monkshood sprawled over the rusted machinery. On the beach two men were shoveling sand down long wooden sluice boxes, "washing" gold.

"Just about manage a day's wage that way," explained our host as we passed. Ahead was a gold dredge in action; the water pipes or "points" plunged deep into the ground to thaw it out before dredging.

The banks, the hotels, the shops, were still there as we rattled over the plank streets of Nome. Empty shells of buildings, many of them, gray, weather-beaten, sagging like an old stage set, tattered banners of a better day. But Nome was still busy. Besides a number of stores selling drugs and provi-sions, there were little shops showing moccasins and ivory work. One large window was a mass of climbing nasturtiums grown from a window box. There were boats coming in, trade and tourists. There was the loading and unloading of lighters in the harbor. That was what brought the King Islanders.

This Eskimo tribe from King Island in the north came to Nome in the summer to get what work they could as longshoremen and, perhaps, selling trinkets to tourists. They paddled eighty miles down the coast in huge "umiaks," walrus-skin boats holding twenty-five or thirty people. When they put to shore they tipped their boats upside down and made tents of them. Here under a curved roof they sat—those of the tribe who were not working in the harbor—and filed away at walrus-tusk ivory, mak-ing bracelets and cigarette holders.

Not today though. Today they were all down at the wharf, as we were, to see their Chief win the kayak race. For, of course, he would win. That was why he was Chief. He was taller and stronger and stood better and danced better and hunted better than anyone else in the tribe. When he ceased to excel, he would cease to be Chief. I wondered, looking at him, if he had to be browner than the rest of them too. He stood quite near us on the dock, shaking his head and sturdy shoulders into a kind of raincoat, a hooded parka made of the gut of seals. His head emerging from the opening showed a streak of white across the dark crop of hair, and, looking at his face, one was shocked to see the same splash of white on the side of brow and cheek, as though the usual Eskimo brown were rubbing off. It was not a birthmark, they told me, but some strange disease which was slowly changing the color of his skin. Would it detract from his superiority or increase it? He seemed quite invincible as he stood there, his broad shoulders thrown back, his head well set. Even his features were stronger than those of his men; firmer mouth, more pronounced cheekbones, unusually deepset eyes. He belonged to those born rulers of the earth.

The three men who were to race squeezed into their kayaks (a native boat entirely sealskin-covered except for a hole where the man sits). Each one then tied the skirt of his parka around the wooden rim of the opening so that no water could enter. Man and boat were one, like Greek centaurs. Then they were launched. A cold rain was driving in our faces and the bay was choppy, but the three kayaks, far more delicately balanced than canoes, rode through the waves like porpoises. It was difficult to follow the race. Sometimes the waves hid a boat from view, or breaking over one, covered it with spray. But the Chief won, of course. The crowd on the beach shouted. He did not come in; merely shook the water from his face and started to turn his kayak over in a side somersault. A little flip with the paddle and he was upside down. "That's how easily they turn over," I thought. For one horrible second the boat bobbed there in the surf, bottom up, like one of those annoying come-back toys with the weight stuck in the wrong end. A gasp from the crowd. Than "A-a-ah!" everyone sighed with relief. He flipped right side up, smiled, shook the water off his face. What was he thinking as he shoved in to shore after that triumph? He had won. He had turned a complete somersault in rough water. No one else could do it as well. He was Chief of the King Islanders.

We saw him again at night. The bare raftered hall was jammed with the Eskimo and white inhabitants of Nome. Around the walls, as in an old-fashioned dancing school, sat a row of Eskimo mothers. Leaning over their calico skirts they peered at the audience and at the same time kept watch of their black-eyed children who sprawled in and out among the slat chairs. There was much giggling and rustling of paper programs. As the curtain rose one noticed first the back wall hung with furs, one huge white bearskin in the center. The stage itself was empty except for a long box, like a large birdhouse, in which were five portholes. On top of the box over each hole squatted an Eskimo in everyday dress: skin trousers, boots, and parka. Out of the holes suddenly popped five wolves' heads. Ears erect, fangs bared, yellow eyes gleaming, the heads nodded at us. Nodded, nodded, nodded, insanely like a dream, this way and that, to the rhythmic beat of a drum. For now in the background of the stage sat some Eskimo women and a few old men chanting and pounding out the rhythm of those heads. Every little while when a head became awry, the Eskimo on top leaned over and jerked it straight by pulling at an ear. The snarling heads began to look childish. Weren't those squatting figures just like the nurses in Central Park? "Tony! Anne! Christopher! Come here—what have you done to your coat? Look where your hat is! There now—go along." They apparently had no part in the drama, these nurses. Like the black-hooded figures who run in and out on the Japanese stage, they were, I assumed, supposed to be invisible, and only there for convenience.

Pound, pound, pound—out of the holes leaped the wolves (who were dressed in long white woolen underwear below their fierce heads). On all fours they stared at us. Pound, pound, pound—they nodded this way, that way, this way, that way, unceasingly, like a child who is entranced with a new trick and cannot shake himself free of it, but repeats it again and again, a refrain to his life. Pound, pound, pound—they were on their feet and shaking their bangled gauntlets this way and that. The wolf in the center tossed his head and glared at us—the Chief of the King Islanders. Pound, pound, pound, the nodding went on and on. Pound, pound, pound, their movements were sudden and elastic, like animals. There was more repose in their movement than in their stillness, which was that of a crouching panther, or a taut bow. One waited, tense, for the inevitable spring. Action was relief. Pound, pound, pound—legs in the air and a backward leap. They had all popped into the holes, disappeared completely. The crosslegged nurses merely nodded approval. And the curtain fell.

The Chief of the King Islanders came out from a door to the left of the stage. The wolf's head lay limp in his hand. Sweat ran down his face. He stood a head above the rest of the group and had that air of being looked at which is quite free from any self-consciousness, as though stares could reflect themselves on the face of the person beheld even when he is unconscious of them. The Chief did not notice the eyes turned toward him, for he was watching the sports now beginning in the hall.

Chairs pushed back, the Eskimo boys were kicking, with both feet together, at a large ball suspended from the rafters. Their toes often higher than their heads, they doubled up in a marvelously precise fashion like a jackknife. Now the girls' competition. The ball was lowered from the ceiling to meet their height. A thin strip of a girl was running down the aisle, her black braids tossing arrogantly. Stop, leap, and kick—the ball shot into the air and spun dizzily. That was an easy one. "The Chief's daughter," someone whispered to me. The ball was raised; the contestants fell out; one fat girl tried and sat down on the floor; everyone laughed.

There were only two left now. A run, a jump, and a leap—the ball floated serenely out of reach. Three times and out. Only the Chief's daughter left. A run, a jump, and a leap—the ball gleamed untouched. She missed it. She ran back shaking her braids. The ball was still. Several people coughed, rustled their programs. I saw her sullen little face as she turned. A run, a jump, and a leap. We could not see her touch it but the ball quivered slightly and began to spin. She had grazed it. "Hi! Hi!" shouted the Eskimos, and the crowd clapped. Her expression did not change as she wriggled back into her seat. But the Chief of the King Islanders was smiling, an easy, arrogant smile.

The next morning we walked down the plank streets of Nome to the King Islanders' camp. The town was quiet after the excitement of the night before. Life in the camp was going on as usual. In the shade of their long curved "umiaks" sat whole families, mothers nursing their babies, old men filing at ivory tusks, while near by were young men curing fish, hanging long lines of them up to dry in the sun. We stopped and talked to one of the ivory filers. He had a half-finished match box in his hand. A pile of white dust lay at his feet. He was, we were to discover, the Chief's brother.

"That was a wonderful dance of yours last night." A broad smile accentuated his high cheekbones. Then gravely he looked up at us.

"My," he said simply.

"'My,'" we echoed. "What do you mean?"

"My," he repeated with emphasis, putting down his file, "*my* brother, *my* son, *my* nephews—" He took a long breath. "*My*"

That was it, I thought, as we walked back. That was what the Chief of the King Islanders felt, shaking the water from his face after the somersault. That was what he thought tossing his wolf's head. That was what he meant by that smile when his daughter made the ball quiver— simply, "My."

IRAAHURUK

Eskimo Folk Tales

The Man-Who-Became-a-Caribou

 ❧

IN WALES (SAGMALARUK) Village there was a man and his wife and their two sons. The woman's mother also lived with them. The man had snares on a hill. Every time the man went out to check them his mother-in-law always said behind his back, "That man has a big bladder." He heard her call him nakasuk̇tuk̇ (big bladder). He began to get tired of her calling him that. When he went out again he heard that name again behind him and he got mad. He went to see his snares and never came

According to her story, Iraahuruk was born in 1880 "on the coast at Ukaliksuk in May when the ice was breaking up. The white men call me Edna Hunnicutt, but my Eskimo name is Iraahuruk." By either name, this story-teller is the most fabled in Eskimo history. Eighty of her tales were recorded in 1965 by anthropologist Edwin S. Hall in The Eskimo Storyteller.

home. Before that they had never been out of food because the man had always hunted.

When he left his snares he walked to the mountain. He heard people laughing. He was climbing up a hill so he got up on top and then went down to see who was laughing. It was ptarmigan making noise just like laughing and talking. He thought that the ptarmigan were people. When he went down the ptarmigan got in one bunch and started eating rocks. He went farther on. As he went around a bend by a little lake he heard people laughing again. He went closer and saw geese fly from the lake.

He went farther on and when he saw some wolves he followed them. When they stopped, he stopped. When they moved on, he moved on. That's how he traveled. One time when the wolves stopped again he stopped a little ways away. The wolves got in a circle and had a meeting. One of the wolves came from the circle toward the man. When it got to him, the wolf put his nose to the ground and pulled his face skin back like pulling a hood back and asked him, "Why do you keep following us?" The man answered, "I want to become a wolf and join you." The wolf went back to the rest of the wolves and after staying with them awhile came back over to the man. When he got back to the man he put his nose to the ground again, pulled his face back, and said: "You want to join us, but my friends say that when it is stormy and we have no food we always eat another wolf. When we see a man hunting and we are short of food we always eat him. Why don't you try to become some other kind of animal and not stay with us?"

When the man decided not to join the wolves he started to follow the caribou. He saw the way the caribou pawed the ground to take the snow off and eat moss. He saw the smaller of the two bones in the front legs (called the needle). He followed the caribou for a year, winter and summer. One time when he was following them a caribou came, put his nose

53

to the ground, pulled his hood back, and asked, "Why have you been following us?" The man answered, "I want to join you." The caribou went
back to the herd where he stayed a little while and then started back
towards the man carrying a caribou skin. When the caribou got to the man
he took his hood off and told the man, "You can put this caribou skin on."
The man put the skin on and he and the caribou sewed it up down the
down the middle of the underside. Then the man tried to walk, but he
always fell. He didn't know how to walk in the skin. The caribou told
him, "If you put your head up and look toward the sky you will probably
start walking." He looked toward the sky and started walking, but still not
very well. He still fell every time he looked down. The caribou told the
man-that-became-a-caribou: "You started walking, so now you stay close
behind me. We always have trouble with people because they hunt us, so
I'll tell you if people come. If I say there is a man coming, stay close behind
me if I start running. Watch closely. If anything happens run ahead. If men
get caribou and don't cut their throats after they kill them, the soul never
comes back."

After awhile the caribou said, "There is a man coming hunting
caribou." The man-who-became-a-caribou looked back at the man coming.
The caribou said, "He's not going to get one of us." The man was carrying a
whole bunch of willows from a house floor. The caribou said, "When he
was little his mother fed him from her breast instead of letting him go out
early in the morning. He's not going to get any of us." The man didn't get
any because the caribou ran away. They saw him because of the dark willows he carried.

When they got together in a big herd again the caribou said,
"There is a man coming again." The caribou saw him coming. They caribou
said, "That man coming has something dark again. Every morning before
that man goes out hunting he puts his hands between his wife's legs and

lays down with her instead of going out early." They ran away again and the man didn't get any [caribou].

The caribou rebunched and started eating from the snow. When they dig down they always get fat from the ground [eat enough to get fat]. You can see it along their stomach. When the caribou saw another hunter he told the man-who-became-a-caribou, "A man is coming. If he gets close to us he's going to kill lots of us." The man-who-became-a-caribou turned around and saw the man as a thin stick, not as a large, dark spot. Before they knew it he was close and he killed lots of caribou. After the rest had run and got together again the caribou said: "When that man was small his mother let him go out early in the morning. But when a hunter never cuts the caribou's throat that caribou never comes home. When a man does cut the throat the soul is like a feather and when it comes back we can see that feather even though the caribou is missing. Some of them are not home because that man didn't cut some of their throats."

In the summertime the man-who-became-a-caribou was always alone. The other caribou went off somewhere. In the fall they got together again. When they did they saw a man coming. They told the man-who-became-a-caribou, but he couldn't see him, and before he knew it a lot of caribou were dead. Then another man came and the caribou said, "There is a man coming." The man-who-became-a-caribou tried to see him, but he couldn't. The caribou said, "He is going to kill a lot of us. If he starts shooting just stay behind me."

The hunter got closer and the caribou went towards him just as if the world was tipping to him. When the caribou started going towards him he killed a lot. The man-who-became-a-caribou and his friend ran away and didn't get caught. This hunter got more caribou than the first one. The caribou said: "That man's mother got him up early in the morning. She told him to take a few pieces of wood to the old men and the old women in the village and put it by their door while they slept. She told him, 'Early in the morning you should always go down to the river and make a hole so people can get water.' That's how this man learned, and after he got older he always gets lots of caribou." All of the caribou the man got came home. They saw their feathers because he cut all their throats.

After the bunch regrouped they stayed together all winter and in the spring they left the man-who-became-a-caribou. He started thinking about where he had put his snares when he was a man. He thought that he should look there, so he went and he recognized the place. While he was looking he stopped all at once. He tried to get out, but he was caught in his own snare. When he couldn't get out he thought to himself, "Somebody must be watching my snare." He put his head down and stayed there waiting for someone to take him out. While he waited he heard men's voices away off. He put his head up and, listening, heard the talking coming towards him. He saw two young boys coming with bows in their hands and arrows on their backs. They got close and he heard them say, "We got a caribou again." They were surprised because they were really too young to hunt.

They got close. One book took an arrow from his back, put it in the bow, and was going to shoot the caribou because he was alive. Just as he was going to shoot, the man put his head to the ground and took his hood off. The boy stopped and the man-who-became-a-caribou said, "Don't be scared of me. Please take the snare off." The boys didn't move, so the man said again, "Don't be scared. Take the snare off." They went to him and took the snare off. After they did the man-who-became-a-caribou said, "I've just got a sewn-on skin on. Take it off." The boys took the stitches out. Before they got it off the man asked, "Whose snares are these?" One boy said, "Our mother always told us they are our father's snares. When he went to see them he never came home." The man told them, "You are my boys. When you grandmother always talked behind me I didn't like it, so I went to see my snares and ran away. Did your mother get married again?" The boys told him she had gotten married. They took his skin off and he had no clothes, so they gave him some of theirs. They had to get ahold of him, one boy grabbing him under each armpit, because he couldn't walk like a man anymore. He walked like a caribou. He told them, "I want to go to the village and tell the people how I ran away." When they took his clothes off one of his shoulders had become that of a caribou.

When they took him home and he went inside the house it smelled of people so much that he couldn't stand it. The man who had married his wife told him, "You came home so you can go back to your wife." He said, "I am not going back to her because I have already become a caribou. Make a house outdoors for me. I'll have a meeting with all the villagers and tell them how I traveled when I went away." They made a house for him. He told the people what he saw when he was with the caribou. He told them how he tried to become a wolf but they didn't want him, and about his mother-in-law and why he had run away. He told the young boys and young girls not to follow his trail, not to do what he had done. After he told them the story he starved because he couldn't eat people's food. THE END.

This is a real true story. Just a few years ago that man down that way became a caribou. I have forgotten where I heard this story.

The Point Hope Boy and the Man-Who-Always-Kills-People

∾

THERE WERE PEOPLE in Point Hope. A rich man there had a son who got all kinds of animals when he hunted. When men hunted in the hills they didn't come home. When they didn't come home the rich man's son tried hunting up that way and he never came home. A grandmother and her grandson lived in Point Hope too. The rich man's son had been liked by that grandson. When the rich man's son didn't come home the grandson went to the rich man and asked him if he had any old snowshoes and a bow and arrow and a spear. The rich man gave the grandson snowshoes, spears, and a bow and arrows. The rich man told the grandson, "Behind the hills there is a flat. Long ago my parents gave me that flat. There is always a lot of caribou up there."

The grandson went up the hill. He saw the flat, but he didn't see caribou even though the rich man said he saw some every time he went up. The grandson walked farther up and he saw a fog bank in front of him. He went to the foggy place and got up on top of a hill. He saw men playing football below him and farther over a house. He went to the house. Inside there was an old man and his wife. The old woman said, "If the man-who-always-kills-people finds out about you he'll call for you. He always takes strangers up to the top of the hill and challenges them to a race. The man-who-always-kills-people stays on the right side because he has a knife in his right arm, and when he reaches the flat he kills the strangers there or takes them to his house and then kills them. When he takes them to his house there is a rock there where he kills men. It has blood and hair on it."

While she was talking a voice came through the window saying, "The stranger has to go over to the man-who-always-kills people." The old woman told the grandson to watch out. The man-who-always-kills-people took him up to the hill to race. He stayed on the right and kept the grandson on the left. The grandson watched him closely. They started racing down

58

the hill. When they got to the flat the man-who-always-kills-people was going to knife him, but the grandson kept away.

When they finished the race the grandson went back to the old couple's house. He went in. After the football game the old couple's three boys came in. Pretty soon two other men came in and said, "The man-who-always-kills-people wants the stranger." The three boys said, "Yes, we'll all go up." The old people said, "We'll go too, so he'll have to kill all of us."

They went up to the man-who-always-kills-people's house. They went to see if the man-who-always-kills-people would kill the grandson. They all wanted to be killed if he killed the grandson. The-man-who-always-kills-people told two of the boys to bring that rock, and they did. It was a real sharp rock with dried blood and men's hair on it. The man-who-always-kills-people went to the grandson, got ahold of him, and whirled him around. He was going to throw him on the rock, but the grandson just missed the sharp edge and landed on his hands and knees on the floor. The grandson said, "You beat me." This happened again.

After the man-who-always-kills-people did this a third time the grandson said, "You are not the only one who's going to go around. Let me try you." He got up and went to the man-who-always-kills-people. He got ahold of him, whirled him around, threw him on the rock, and killed him. After he killed the man-who-always-kills-people he said, "Anybody that's thinking about my killing this man-who-always-kills-people come on down." Nobody came down. The grandson and his friends went home. He stayed for a year and then went back to Point Hope. The Point Hopers said, "If there was still a man-who-always-kills-people up there, Point Hopers wouldn't come home even now if the grandson hadn't killed him." THE END.

I heard this story from Paul Monroe today. Paul forgets where he heard it. [Paul said, "Edna told this story right through even though she only heard it once. Everything was right."]

The Woman and the Eagle

ON POINT HOPE there lived two older people with a son. On the north side of the village lived a woman with no husband. Behind Point Hope there was a big karigi, or meeting place. The Point Hope man always went up to the karigi when they were going to have a meeting. Every time he came home he told his wife that whenever he put his mittens on, in order to go, the kids always talked to him and let him stay a few hours. Whenever he came home he told his wife that again, but every evening he stayed longer.

Finally, when he was going again, she was suspicious and followed him. She found out that he went to the widow's house on the north side of the village. When he came home late again it was daylight. He told her the same story. He went out the next night and she followed again and saw him go to the widow again. Her heart broke right there. This happened another night and she started to think that she will get a seal skin and make a boat cover. [Edna used the word for dried seal skin; the translator remarked that it must be winter or spring.] When her husband came home she always put her sewing away so he couldn't see. She sewed with small, waterproof stitches. Finally she started making the boat. She finished and put a string to tie the boat above her head (some kind of round boat).

She started thinking that the wind should be from the east [to drive the ice away from shore]. She went out from the house one morning before her husband came home and saw open water. She went back inside. The second time she came out she saw more open water, so she went and got her boat. She put the boy on her back and went down toward the ocean. When she got to the beach someone yelled "Akham" (wait for me). It was her husband, but she wouldn't wait, saying he should have said "Akham" long ago, before he visited that woman.

When she got to open water she put the boat down, got inside with the boy, and tied it up. She knew the waves would take them away from the shore. She didn't know where they were heading. They had no food. All summer she spent on the water, her child crying for food, but they had none and he got skinny. Finally they stopped, as if the water couldn't move them anymore, and she tried to rock the boat, but she couldn't. So she opened the boat and saw ground.

After she opened the boat they both got out. She couldn't stand, so she put the boy on her back and started to crawl. She saw a little lake. She crawled there and started cleaning her boy and herself. There was ahnuk all over her back. Then they rested until she began to feel stronger.

She got up and started walking along the beach. Farther on she saw a house with two high inusuks (meat caches, also called ikigut). One was filled with beluga and one with black whale. When she got to the house she stood outside for awhile and then went in. She saw only one parka hanging in the stormshed. It was a long parka. She stayed in the stormshed for awhile, then went into the house. It was obvious that there was only one person living there. Food was ready. She went to the corner and sat down, putting her baby on her stomach under the parka. There was lots of food around, but she was scared to eat.

She heard someone outdoors. A man came in and said, "You poor thing." Then he said, "Why didn't you try to eat when you came in? The food is all for you. Put your baby down and feed us." She cooked and they started eating. The man started liking the boy when he saw him. They stayed together and the man didn't want to let her go. He started hunting. When he came home he'd have one-half beluga. He'd also bring home black whale.

The boy kept getting bigger. Finally he got big and wanted to hunt also. The man started taking him along, putting the parka in the shed on him. Every time they got beluga and black whale. The man started telling the boy not to try to kill the black whale that spit out red flames.

When the boy got older, he started thinking, "Why doesn't father want me to get the black whale that spits out red flame?" He saw the black whale that spit out red flame and got ahold of him by turning into an eagle (the man was an eagle when out hunting). The boy got his claws into the whale and got stuck there. He couldn't get loose. While he was trying to get free the water came up to his waist, so he began to call for his father. When the water got up to his neck his father came and pulled him off the whale. After that the boy didn't hunt the black whale that spit out red flame. The woman and the boy stayed for a long time and the old man couldn't talk much anymore. Sometimes he didn't say a word in the evening. Finally he didn't speak for a long time. Finally he said that he started hearing the boy's true father's voice.

The boy flew away again looking for his real home. He started seeing kayaks with seals or ugruks lashed to them. He recognized Point Hope so he started flying close to the kayaks until he recognized his father's kayak. The kayaks started home full speed when they saw the eagle. The boy started flying close to his father. He flew above him, got very close, and then would turn and his father's kayak would try to tip. His father started yelling for help.

When they got close to the houses the eagle started his diving again and the man in the kayak yelled louder. Finally the boy clawed his father in the shoulder and picked him up, kayak and all. He flew low over the houses. He dropped his father somewhere in the mountains. Then he went home to his mother and stepfather. His stepfather said something when he went in the house. He said to the boy's mother that when he found out that the boy's true father went to the widow, the eagle knew and pitied that woman and boy, so he took her mind and made her ready to make the boat and get in it. He made her go away. The man and the woman forgave each other. THE END.

I heard this story from Ralph Gallahorn.

LARRY GALLAGHER

The Young Men and the Sea

THE ELBOW ROOM was crawling, as it always does on a Saturday night, a giant crab pot packed with unsavory-looking creatures in woolly beards and baseball caps, scuttling back and forth through the smoke and the din. Fresh off the jet from Anchorage, I slipped in and found a stool off to one side of the bar. A scraggly quartet of musicians were insisting that they were knocking on heaven's door, and they were making a good case for themselves. I sat there in lumberjack shirt, jeans, and regulation gum boots, nursing a Rainier and trying to look as inconspicuous as possible.

Larry Gallagher is a footloose adventurer and contributing editor to
Details *magazine. He lasted one summer fishing in Kodiak and recorded his experiences in "The Young Men and the Sea," which first appeared in* Details *in 1991.*

Within five minutes I was approached by a man who looked like a cross between Jerry Garcia and a grizzly bear, maybe a little hairier than both, with thick glasses, love beads, and a black bear tooth hanging around his neck on a quarter-inch polypropylene line.

"Uh, 'scuze me," he said, smiling shyly. "Me and the boys were just trying to figure out what kind of scientist you were." Over his shoulder I noticed an especially dog-eared contingent eyeing me from a booth in the corner. I explained the nature of my visit. "I'm Snarl," he said, extending a hand. "Why don't you come meet the boys?" I followed him across the room. "This is Caveman, and this is Manimal, this is Todd, that's Father Guacamole over there." I sat down next to a guy who introduced himself as Fred, crushed my hand, and stared coldly and silently into my eyes for three or four long seconds. "Welcome to Dutch Harbor."

You don't end up in Dutch by accident. At least not a single accident. A string of bad choices might land you on her beaches, or you might be flown in on any number of different missions. But no wrong turn will bring you to this rock at the top of the Pacific, this link in the 1,100-mile chain of mountains known as the Aleutians. Dutch Harbor is a terminus, the last industrial outpost of the Alaskan fisherman, the playground of the earth's last great hunter-gatherers, and the last refuge for all the human wildlife that drifts westward on the current. Out here there is still some meaning left in the big Alaskan metaphors of frontier and gold rush; Dutch is still a place where men go to prove themselves or lose themselves, a place that offers high odds of adventure and rewards those who survive it.

"Yeah," warned one veteran, "there are a lot of wild children running around out there."

Wild children of all ages end up in the Elbow Room. I'd heard it was one of the toughest bars in the country, a judgment supported by the reinforced Plexiglas window in the corner, designed to discourage its use as an exit in the likely event of a brawl. "We don't make a big deal about it," said Fred. "If there's a problem, we go outside and arbitrate with our fists, then come back in and have a drink." Fred had warmed up decidedly once he found out that I wasn't a "narc" for the federal fish police and even told me his real name, which was Bert. Bert was something of a spokesman for the bunch, possibly because he also happened to have the longest beard, a red ZZ Top model streaked with gray. His nose had a slightly expressionist bend to it, a reminder of the time when, having returned from 'Nam, he found out that he wasn't the "baddest motherfucker on the face of the earth." Years of chain-smoking had turned his hands into nicotine-brown claws, like those of the tanner crab he'd spent much of the last sixteen years pursuing. "We are the keepers of the progressive value of fishing, and we're feeding half the earth." Bert led the evening's program of half-audible, half-credible fish stories, tales of hurricanes and shipwrecks, brawls and furiously spent crew shares. When somebody else was telling a story he'd hop out of the booth to dance a gallant two-step with one of the local matrons who'd stopped in for a drink, the only females in evidence.

At the end of the long, drunken evening Bert insisted that I would be remiss in my research if I didn't crash for a night at his cabana. "It's a home for wayward souls, the last one on the whole island," declared Bert. "I'm the last of the lowlifes in scum gully."

At four in the morning the last of the drunks were kicked out of the Elbow Room and into the waiting taxi-vans. Bert and I climbed in with Father Guacamole, a beatific Deadhead and retired acid priest from Berkeley who was driving the night shift. "Guatemala" was actually the name he had conceived for himself, but that proved a bit too esoteric for Dutch and was quickly modified for him. He was hoping to get a job crabbing in the fall. In the meantime he had earned enough cabbing to buy a $350 limited-edition buck knife, which he was sending to Jerry Garcia as an enticement to get him to come up and play the Elbow Room.

Bert owned a one-room wooden shack left over from the Second World War. There were already four lost souls, in varying states of deterioration, sitting in the light of a single candle. Bert put on a tape of the Guess Who's greatest hits, which played over and over on a warbly cassette player, while he nibbled on raw hamburger meat from a shopping bag and discoursed on the nature of manliness until everyone had either climbed into the loft to sleep or passed out on the floor.

WHEN I ROLLED out of the cabana the next morning, I could see what Bert meant. The hills surrounding his shack were filling up with million-dollar suburban duplexes of aluminum and glass, the visible confirmation of the latest gold rush that was changing the face of the town. The extension of our territorial waters to two hundred miles served to squeeze the Russian and Japanese fleets away from all the good underwater shelves, and the American fleet has moved in to clean up. In the process, Dutch Harbor has become the biggest-volume fishing port in the U.S. Every jet that lands, every million-gallon fuel tank that is emptied, every Cat that tears into the side of a hill, every Japanese freighter that appears in the bay, is riding on the backs of dead fish, part of a grand scheme by which complex amino acids are extracted from the sea and sent to become parts of the bodies of humans thousands of miles away.

The walk back to town was like a walk through a 360-degree diorama made up of haphazardly receding planes. Snow-covered volcanoes sat between green, treeless lumps, and clouds were alternately revealing and concealing pieces of the view. Dutch sits on a small island five hundred feet off the larger island of Unalaska ("un" as in "unreal"), about a third of the way out the chain. Unalaska's peaks act like a shredder for two major weather systems from the Bering and Pacific, so the sky is always full of weather. Beneath this strange sky our national symbol, the ever-scavenging eagle, roosts on the propeller of a wind generator looking for an unlucky house cat upon which to sup.

IT WAS THE time of year when the long-line fleet was arriving in Dutch, small boats from all over the Alaskan coast and from as far south as Fort Bragg, California, slowly filling up the harbor, tying up three and four deep on the piers and at the cannery docks. Among fishermen, long-liners—so named for the device they employ to coax fish off the ocean floor—are probably the truest heirs to the old-time spirit of fishing, the last of the independent, small-time warriors. "Crabbers might be stronger than we are," declared a proud long-liner, "but we more than make up for it in orneriness." The restrictions on the fish that they earn their living off of have turned them into a nomadic bunch, keeping them on the move between the Bering Sea and southeastern Alaska in pursuit of "openings."

It takes a certain kind of rugged, twisted individual to be able to tolerate the endless hours of baiting, hauling, and deep-water surfing required of the trade. By comparison, the lifestyle of the salmon fishermen, who fish a short summer season in daylight, with nets, directly offshore, seems almost genteel. "You spend all your time untangling all them lines and all them hooks," says one long-liner. "Now, that can't be good for a person's disposition, can it?"

Meet Big Wave Dave. Perhaps no one exemplifies this range of qualities as well as this young man from Coeur d'Alene, Idaho. When I met him on the docks he was joining a few of his buddies for a mid-morning joint. "You know how I got this name?" he asked between hits. "See, when I get into town I'm riding on the top of the wave, and after a few days I'm down in the trough." The last time he was in Dutch he was drunk for seven straight days, passing out the first five. Every night he would find himself a job only to lose it the next day when he failed to wake up. "My problem is I can't have one beer."

That afternoon Dave had a beer. Sometime between then and the next sunrise he launched a surprise bottle-rocket attack on the neighboring vessels, vociferously disputed the manliness of a large group of Russian sailors docked nearby, and ripped the wooden door off the wheelhouse of the boat. By the following afternoon Dave was firmly established in the trough. His crew mates were having trouble tracking down the cat. "If he drowned the cat, that's it," said Cal. "He's definitely off the boat." Cal and Paul, his skipper, were trying to figure out a way to sneak past Dave, who had been eighty-sixed from the bar in the UniSea Inn and was stalking like a rabid dog, bumming beer money off unlucky friends and crying that none of his crew mates loved him. "If we could only figure out some way to get him thrown in jail," mused Paul hopefully. "They should open up a court here. They'd make a lot of money." They spotted Dave and tore off behind the surimi-processing center.

"You! I'm gonna kill you!" shouted Big Wave, rushing up to me and grabbing me by the shirt. "Look what that fucking cat did to me." He had gashes all over his wrists and arms. "I was only trying to pet it." I asked him if I could go out with his boat for the next opening. "No. Impossible. You just walk around saying, 'I'm a writer, I'm a writer.' I'm a better writer than you are. Got any money?"

Luckily, a cab happened to be passing by and Big Wave Dave took off after it, barking, "Hey! I'm gonna kill you!"

I WAS TRYING to track down Jim Webber, a long-lining legend whose name kept popping up. "He's got the last of the old hippie pirate boats, notorious from here to Homer. He's as crazy as they come," said one fisherman who'd just gotten back to Dutch. Said another, "Lots of good men got their start with Webber. Some people say that if you haven't long-lined with Webber you haven't long-lined yet. You should go for a ride with him; he'll tell you a story or two." I was told that Webber was the skipper of a blue steel forty-two-footer called the *Spectrum*, and I headed down to the docks to track him down.

The docks were starting to come to life. The smell of old fish blood and burnt diesel filled the air, new additions mixing with the barnacle-and-seawater smell of the dock and the sharp smells of decay wafting over from the cannery. The boats are as varied as the men working them, old wooden schooners from before the First World War, modern fiberglass bathtubs, and a lot of fifty-foot steel beaters built sometime in between. The names tend toward bland, white-bread, girl, names (*Donna C., Jani K.*), intermingled with the boneheadedly macho (*Terminator, Survivor*), lightened occasionally by the humorous (*Lani Ru*—"urinal" spelled backward—or *Flying Usig*, Aleut for the male member of a sea lion). On the back decks of boats, the crews worked at a lazy pace, untwisting strings of gear or baiting, to the sounds of Megadeth and Hank Williams Jr., getting ready for the opening a week away.

It didn't take long to find the whereabouts of Webber. He was on the floor of the Bering Sea, somewhere off the coast of Atka, four hundred miles out the chain. I found this out inadvertently when I ran into Todd, whom I had met my first night at the Elbow Room. "He went down on the *Betty B* last month," he said, looking down at his boots. "I was on that boat." The boat had drifted onto a reef off Atka and started taking on water. Todd managed to get into his neoprene survival suit, but the *Betty B* rolled before his two crew mates could escape with theirs. Todd had watched as the other two were sucked down with the boat. "Yeah, well, I don't really want to talk about it," he said as he walked away.

Death is a major industry in Dutch. Crushed by 760-pound crab pots, squeezed to death by huge steel doors on processors, decapitated by flying anchors, the bodies pass through the airport on their way south. Some get caught in lines and dragged into the water. Others simply go out in the back of a moving boat to take their last pee and never come back, remaining mysteries until their bodies wash ashore with dicks hanging unceremoniously out of their raingear. Every year boats disappear without a trace, and bodies turn up in trawl nets and on the beaches of Siberia.

"You get a lot of guys who come up for a season. Some of 'em don't go home," cackles Eddie, the forty-six-year-old skipper of the crabbing boat *Mahalo*. "You know how it is, life in the food chain. They become dinner for some giant king crab down there. One day I'll be eating a big piece of king crab and I'll say, 'Eh, tastes like George.' " He breaks down in maniacal laughter.

Death is an inescapable reality up here; whether this is true of taxes is open for debate. Earl, nearly thirty years old, has been fishing for a decade, averaging about $45,000 a year and making twice that in his best season. He's managed to spend every bit of it without spilling a dime into the coffers of the IRS. "I figure I owe them bastards $100,000 by now." Mort has found a different solution to his problem: he's been dead since 1978. "Yeah, I think old Mort went down on a boat somewhere," I was told with a wink and a grin. "They never did find the body." Mort still returns to the Aleutians to fish each summer, no slim feat for a man in his condition.

Mort is not the only soul in Dutch with a past worth fleeing. The question "Where are you from?" is considered bad manners. "Nobody cares who you were," says one longtime resident. The distance from the country is echoed in the terms used to refer to it: "Down south," "Outside," and "the States." Every month the police blotter in the *Aleutian*

Eagle is filled with the names of fugitives picked up on old warrants. But given the considerable cost of extradition—the fare between Anchorage and Dutch alone being one of the most expensive per-mile jet fares in the country—no small town in Missouri is going to pay to have a problem shipped back.

THE ALASKA FISHING fleet is an archipelago of floating islands, a small town spread out over hundreds of sea miles, operating with its own rules and principles on a plane of reality that only occasionally intersects that of the rest of the world. Crews rearrange themselves and boats change hands with such frequency that it is often the vessels themselves that provide the only continuity from year to year. Society's systems of time-keeping—the movement of the sun, the sleeping and waking cycles of the human body, the passing of the seasons—are replaced by the dictates of fish and finance, and people stop you on the docks to ask you what day it is.

Fishing also has its own social hierarchies, a caste system based on the earning potential and the relative pain involved in the labor. In Dutch, crabbers supply the standard by which courageousness and craziness are judged. They make their living in the dead of winter, emptying 750-pound roach motels of steel and web and earning anywhere up to $100,000 for a few months on the water. Long-liners and trawlers, who can earn $45,000 in a good season, vie for the next spot on the social ladder. The small trawlers like to distinguish between themselves and the behemoth catcher-processors, but both catch cod and pollock in large funnel-shaped nets that they drag behind them, and both are despised by the long-liners, who contend that "draggers" are killing off everything in their path and ripping up the ocean floor. "I'd rather have a sister in a whorehouse," goes the not-so-old adage, "than a brother on a dragger." At the bottom of the pile are processors, a.k.a. "slimers," the invisible hands who man the floating

71

factories out in the Bering. Work on a "slave ship" gutting cod or packing crab is dull and repetitive, but there's usually plenty of it, six hours on and six hours off around the clock. And if there are no fish to catch, the fishermen still get their $6.50 an hour.

Money remains the primary lure enticing people to come to Dutch. But once they get here, it starts playing tricks on them. There are plenty of fishermen who make their stash quietly, take it back home, and invest it wisely, the prudent boats that blow in and out of town as quickly as possible. But in the gold rush the value of money is easily lost, and many are the souls who have drunk and snorted away every last bit of their diggings. Expectation is skewed by jackpots—the legendary $40,000 crew share for two weeks of crabbing, the $8,000 take for forty-eight hours of halibut fishing. As happens in other forms of gambling, the jackpot becomes everything, and the dream that makes it possible is forgotten. To burn money is to show contempt for and freedom from the power it holds over men. Above the bar in the Elbow Room is a bell which, when rung, entitles the ringer to buy a round for the house. "I've run that bell eight times in one night," Bert had boasted. "Money means nothing to me. I make it fast and I spend it fast."

The scent of fresh money is in the air in Dutch as the long-liners are scurrying around, getting the last bit of bait or fuel or ice before they leave town. The unemployed walk the docks, hoping to secure a job before it's too late. The lines grow longer at the pay phones in front of the UniSea, and every last bit of red meat is gone from the grocery store. One by one the boats slip out of town, off to the halibut banks to try their luck and test their will.

"THERE IS NO drug," says one lifelong warrior, "that can get you as high as halibut fishing." For pure, sustained intensity of kill, there is nothing in the industry to rival it. To keep the species from being completely annihilated, the International Pacific Halibut Commission opens the season only a few days a year, giving the fisherman twenty-four or forty-eight hours to rake in all he can. For the fleet assembled in Dutch Harbor, a lot will be riding on those few hours. Boats will head west along the Aleutian chain our out as far as Adak and as far north as the island of St. Matthew, three hundred miles into the Bering Sea. At the stroke of noon on the designated day, they'll run their lines off the back of the boat. At the end of each line will be a buoy and an anchor, one to help the line get down to the ocean floor and the other to get it back again. Once the killing starts there will be no respite for man or beast. Halibut, cantankerous flatfish that grow regularly to two to three hundred pounds, will be drawn up from the bottom of the ocean on a hydraulic winch. When they reach the surface they will be greeted with a steel hook in the skull from the man at the roller, then dragged over the rail onto the deck. Invective will rain as angry fishermen attempt to subdue flopping halibut by clubbing their heads with baseball bats, ax handles, or steel pipes. Blood will flow and organs will fly as the fish are lugged onto the cutting tables, where they are hastily relieved of gills, guts, and gonads. Down in the cramped hold of the boat, men will crawl around on all fours in semidarkness, dragging fish carcasses over their bodies and filling the freshly eviscerated bellies with chipped ice. All through the night and back again into the day, behind the grind of hydraulics, on an ever-shifting stage, the drama will unfold in a blur of fish blood and slime.

AFTER A FEW days, boats are back in Dutch unloading their catch. And their cash. Taxi-vans shuttle back and forth between the Elbow Room and the UniSea, where wired fishermen are re-creating the frenzy of fishing. The bottom feeders are out in full force, too. As with any gold rush, it's not always the miners who end up with the most money, but those who mine the miners. Word is that it takes fifteen minutes to find coke, about as long as it takes to ride from one side of the island to the other. The flesh merchants are in town, the $200-a-throw professionals who fly in from Anchorage and Seattle to ride the seasonal peaks.

When I first met Paul he was joyriding on a Sunday night in the back of a taxi-van, a cheap source of entertainment in a town with no cheap entertainment. He was quick to let me know that he had been an architecture student—Virginia Polytechnic—in the life he left behind. When he came up to Alaska in May he was looking to pay off a few school debts. Like thousands of his peers, Paul, twenty-three, drove across the country on the hope that he'd make a pile of money working on a fishing boat. Unlike most of them, who end up working in canneries or stranded on the beach, Paul actually found a fishing job long-lining for cod on a boat out of Kodiak. "It was the first time I experienced utter misery. The crew was evil. The weather was horrible. I got seasick and thought I was going to die. And we didn't catch any fish." His second trip was better. The sun was out, the seas were calm, and they ran into a pod of sperm whales on the way back to town. "I was hooked." After that he caught a lift on a boat that was heading out to Dutch, where he crossed paths with Kyle, whom he'd known from architecture school and who got him a job on the *Semidi*, a classic old wooden long-liner out of Seattle.

A few days later, when I tracked down the *Semidi*, Paul gave me the rest of the story. The truth was, after a season in Alaska, the world was starting to look a little different. He wasn't sure he was in such a rush to get a job in an architect's office. Not that he wanted to spend his life fishing. "It's too unhealthy," he insisted. "It makes you animal-like, and it ages you really quickly." Still, this summer he managed to gross $8,000 on greenhorn shares. If he comes back to fish for the *Semidi* next spring, his percentage will double. Already he was beginning to wonder how he would fit back into the routines of his old life. "I don't know," he said. "It's going to be hard to go back."

He won't be the first to find this out. Scott started to realize as much ten years ago, when he began fishing in Alaska. "At first I came for the adventure," admitted the thirty-three-year-old "immigrant" from Minnesota when I met him at the mess hall. "The water is a never-ending form of psychological warfare." Now he's hooked into it because of the money. "Every time I fish halibut I tell myself, 'Never again.' You get carpal tunnel, tennis elbow." But after a decade on the warrior circuit, quitting, he's found, can be quite tough. "You decide to stay home with your old lady for an opener, and then all your buddies come back to town all excited, loaded with fish, and you feel like a coward for giving up." After two bad seasons the trap is tighter, but he's praying for one good season that will give him enough capital to buy himself a "puker boat" and start leading fishing charters. "I'm going to go after the tourist dollar instead of the black-and-blue dollar. I just hope I can get out before the whole thing collapses."

That is the hope and fear of everyone in Dutch Harbor. For the long-liners, the handwriting is on the wall, and they are not alone in pinning the blame on the factory trawlers. "It's over," said Scott. "They're the same people who killed the buffalo. The same thing happened on the East Coast. They're raping the ocean and ripping up the substrate, and when they're done they'll move to another part of the world and start all over again."

"Adapt, Migrate, or Die" is the motto of the trawlers, who deny everything. What has them a little worried is the shrinking size of pollock, the plentiful white fodder fish, turned into surimi and Filet-O-Fish, which brings in billions. "The fact is," admitted an observer for the National Marine Fishery Service in hushed tones, "nobody knows how much pollock is out there." With aquaculture growing so quickly, it should be no time at all before king crab and halibut are raised on farms, like chickens and cows, and mankind's last hunter-gatherers will be a thing to tell your grandchildren about. "I keep having a recurring vision," says Dave, a third-generation Alaskan. "I see sheet metal, flapping in the wind."

THERE WAS STILL one puzzle I had to solve for myself before I could leave. I still couldn't understand why so many people would endure so much for so long, only to abandon the reward when they got it. I stuck it to *Mahalo* Eddie, who after over twenty years in the business was still hovering around the zero mark. "Hell, it ain't the money," said Eddie. "It's the independence. If I don't like your ass I can climb over that rail there and never have to look at you again. If I don't like this place I can throw my lines aboard and split. You can't put a price on that kind of freedom."

"You wanna know why we work so hard?" asked Cindy, one of a few female fishermen. Her boat, the *King and Winge*, had just gotten back from the forty-eight-hour opener with 30,000 pounds of halibut in its hold and Cindy was standing over a pile of salted herring heads in the back of the boat. "When you work this hard you don't have time to think about what you're feeling. You don't have time for all those displaced, misplaced feelings. You can't think about all the things you're afraid of, all the things you're running away from. You can dissociate yourself from family or single relationships or trouble with the law or not fitting in anywhere else. We're afraid of things every day. In some ways we have more fear than anybody else."

THE WILLIWAWS THAT earned the Aleutians the nickname "birthplace of the winds" started to blow, whipping through town like furies, as if to clean it of all the stale smoke and bad karma left behind by the long-liners. Most of the small fleet had headed east to Kodiak for the last opening of the season. Things would be quiet for a few weeks until the crabbers started appearing. Bert was sitting in a coffee shop smoking a cigarette, waiting for the Elbow Room to open. He told me Father Guacamole was off in the town hall trying to change his name to "Lovechrist." Big Wave Dave, appearing a little sheepish, was pounding the docks looking for a new job. Todd wasn't looking too good, either. His latest boat had lost a twenty-one-year-old Mexican kid, who disappeared somewhere off the back of the boat during the opener. The eight hits of acid Todd had dropped the night before didn't manage to revive his spirits. I suspected he didn't really want to talk about it.

I was probably projecting, but the wind and the light seemed to be mumbling something about "home." I asked Eddie one last time if he was headed that way. "Home? This is it. My idea of home is walking down some dark, wet dock somewhere at two o'clock in the morning, half-soused, smelling of fish guts. That's home for me."

WILLIAM H. DALL

Alaska and Its Resources

ON MONDAY, THE 1st of October, 1866, the *Nightingale* sailed for Plover Bay. All was activity on shore, preparing the *Wilder* and all available boats for a trip to Unalaklík, the seaboard terminus of the portage to the Yukon, at the mouth of the Unalaklík River. My friend, Mr. Whymper, the genial and excellent artist of the expedition, proposed to leave for Unalaklík on the steamer.

The work of construction and exploration had been divided. The larger number of men, and the work to be done in the region west of the Yukon, had been placed in charge of Mr. W. H. Ennis and several assistants. Here the work of exploration had been mainly finished, and construction, exclusive of putting up the wires, was to be immediately commenced.

William Dall was the director of the Scientific Corps of the Western Union Telegraph Expedition. Fortunately, he also had a flair for writing and kept an extensive, amusing journal of his 1870 Yukon trip, Alaska and Its Resources *(1870).*

The work of exploration and future construction, to the north and east of Nuláto on the Yukon, was intrusted to Mr. F. E. Ketchum, to whom, with Mr. Michael Lebarge, the honor of exploring the region between Nuláto and Fort Yukon had fallen after Kennicott's death.

Mr. Ketchum, who bore the title of Captain in the service of the Expedition, was thoroughly qualified for the execution of the trust committed to him. He had been eminently faithful to Mr. Kennicott during his arduous explorations, and had successfully carried out his plans after his death.

I proposed to accompany him to Nuláto, the place best suited for the prosecution of the scientific work, and as he had decided to remain for a while at St. Michael's, after consultation with him, we secured a room in the Russian quarters together.

On Tuesday the steamer, in charge of Captain E. E. Smith, with a Russian pilot, started for Unalaklík. As we were waving our congratulations, to our dismay we saw her come to a stand-still, plump on a rock at the entrance of the cove. It seemed as if her career were about to come to an ignominious conclusion, but after a good deal of labor she worked off without damage, and proceeded on her way.

THE INMATES OF the fort—with the exception of Sérgei Stepánoff Rúsanoff, an old soldier, who commands not only this, but all the trading-posts in the District of St. Michael, under the title of Uprovalísha—may be divided into three classes: convicts, creoles, and natives.

The workmen of the Russian American Company were, almost without exception, convicts, mostly from Siberia, where the Company was originally organized. They were men convicted of such crimes as theft, incorrigible drunkenness, burglary, and even manslaughter. These men, after a continued residence in the country, naturally took to themselves wives, after the fashion of the country, such Russian subjects in the Company's employ were prohibited from legal marriage with native women. These connections are looked upon with a different feeling from that which prevails in most communities, and these native women mix freely with the few Russian and half-breed women in the territory who have been legally married. Their children are termed creoles, and formerly were taken from their parents and educated in Sitka by the Company, in whose service they were obliged to pass a certain number of years, when they became what is called "free creoles," and were at liberty to continue in the service or not, as they liked. Many of the most distinguished officers of the Company were creoles, among them Étolin, Kushewároff, and Málakoff.

There are a few Yakúts in the service of the Company, and these, with some native workmen, who are generally of the tribe which inhabits the immediate vicinity of the post, compose the garrison.

The regular workman gets about fifty pounds of flour, a pound of tea, and three pounds of sugar, a month; his pay is about twenty cents a day. Some of the older men get thirty cents and a corresponding addition to the ration of flour. They work with little energy and spirit as a general thing, but can accomplish a great deal if roused by necessity. Small offenses are punished by confinement in the guard-house, or *boofka*, and greater ones by a thrashing administered by the commander in person; those who commit considerable crimes are forced to run the gauntlet, receive one or two hundred blows with a stick, or in extreme cases are sent for trial to Sitka, or, in case of murder, to St. Petersburg.

The present Uprovalísha, Stepánoff, has been in office about four years. He is a middle-aged man of great energy and iron will, with the Russian fondness for strong liquor and with ungovernable passions in certain directions. He has a soldier's contempt for making money by small ways, a certain code of honor of his own, is generous in his own

way, and seldom does a mean thing when he is sober, but nevertheless is a
good deal of a brute. He will gamble and drink in the most democratic
way with his workmen, and bears no malice for a black eye when
received in a drunken brawl; but woe to the unfortunate who infringes
discipline while he is sober, for he shall certainly receive his reward; and
Stepánoff often says of his men, when speaking to an American, "You
can expect nothing good of this rabble: they left Russia because they
were not wanted there."

The commanders, or *bidárshiks*, of the smaller posts in the
District of St. Michael are appointed by Stepánoff, who has absolute
authority over them, and does not fail to let them understand it, making
them row his boat, when the annual supply-ship is in port, as
Alexander might have called his captive kings to do him menial service. But Stepánoff trembles before the captain of the ship or an old
officer of the Company, much in the same way that his workmen cringe
before him. This sort of subserviency, the fruit of a despotic government, is characteristic of the lower classes of Russians; and to such an
extent is it ingrained in their characters that it seems impossible for
them to comprehend any motives of honor or truthfulness as being
superior to self-interest.

The native inhabitants of this part of the coast belong to the great
family of *Innuit*. The name of the tribe is *Únaleet*, and their name for the village, half a mile west of the Redoubt on the island of St. Michael, is *T' sat-
súmi*. The few families living there bear the local designation of *Tutsógemut*,
much as we should say Bostonian or New-Yorker. The village comprises
half a dozen houses and a dance-house, built in the native fashion; that is to
say, half underground, with the entrance more or less so, and the roof furnished with a square opening in the centre, for the escape of smoke and
admission of light.

They are built of spruce logs, without nails or pins, and are usually about twelve or fifteen feet square. The entrance is a small hole through which one must enter on hands and knees, and is usually furnished with a bear or deer skin or a piece of matting to exclude the air. Outside of this entrance is a passage-way, hardly larger, which opens under a small shed, at the surface of the ground, to protect it from the weather.

They are about eight feet high in the middle, but the eaves are rarely more than three or four feet above the ground. The floor is divided by two logs into three areas of nearly equal size, the entrance being at the end of the middle one. This portion of the floor is always the native earth, usually hardened by constant passing over it. In the middle, under the aperture in the roof, the fire is built, and here are sometimes placed a few stones. On either side the portion separated by the logs before mentioned is occupied as a place to sit and work in during the day, and as a sleeping-place during the night. The earth is usually covered with straw, or spruce branches when obtainable, and over this is laid a mat woven out of grass. Sometimes the space is raised, or a platform is built of boards, or logs hewn flat on one side. This is a work of such labor, however, that it is seldom resorted to. The beds, which generally consist of a blanket of dressed deerskin, or rabbit-skins sewed together, are rolled up and put out of the way during the day. Almost all sorts of work are done in the houses after the cold weather sets in. At this time, however, there did not appear to be any people in the village, and Captain Ketchum told me that they would not return for a week or two, being absent at Pastólik, where they were killing the beluga or white whale. A solitary old woman, perhaps of exceptional ugliness, spent her time picking berries, which were abundant near the village.

MONDAY, 8TH.—THE weather being clear and fine, the wind nearly fair, we determined to put off to Unalaklík. We left St. Michael's about noon, Westdahl leading, but the wind hauling ahead we ran closer in, and left him making a long tack, which Ketchum was rather apprehensive would be unsuccessful, as it is impossible, or almost so, to beat against the wind with one of these flat-bottomed skin boats.

About eight o'clock P.M. we put into a small rocky cove about twenty-two miles from the Redoubt. This, from two small rocky islets which protect it, is known to the Únaleets as *Kegiktówruk*, a word derived from *kikhtuk*, meaning an island. There is quite a village on the high bank back of the cove, and the inhabitants came down and helped us to haul our boat up on a sort of ways, built of round logs, held in place by large masses of rock. These are necessary, as the cove is very shallow and so full of rocks that the skin boats are very liable to be cut on them at low tide. There were no signs of the other boats.

The village is notable on account of the number of graves scattered over the plain about it, and also for the large size of the dance-house, or *casíne* as the Russians term it. This building is to be found in almost every village, and serves for a general workroom, a sort of town-hall, a steam bath-house, a caravanserai for travellers, and a meeting-house for celebrating their annual dances and festivals.

It is usually the largest and cleanest house in the village, and generally empty at night, so that travellers prefer it to one of the smaller and more dirty and crowded houses. In the present case we were quartered in it very comfortably.

We immediately sent out our teakettle, in this country always made of copper, and universally known as the *chýnik*,—tea being *chy* in the Russian, a derivative from the original Chinese *chah*.

Chy being ready, we imbibed deeply, and filling up the *chýnik* with water we dispensed the diluted fluid to our native friends, in the bountiful tin cups provided by the Company. A small handful of broken biscuit added to the acceptability of the treat and disguised the weakness of the chy. This is the invariable and expected tribute to the hospitality of the natives from all travellers who avail themselves of the casine and other accommodations of the village; for which the Innuit have not yet learned to charge by the night's lodging.

Appreciating the banquet, and warmed to enthusiasm by the hot water, an old bear-eyed individual seized an article something between a drum and a tambourine, and began to beat upon it with a long elastic rod. He was joined by all the old men in the vicinity, in a dismal chorus of

Ung hi yáh, ah ha yáh, yah yah yáh, &c.,

keeping time upon his drum with an energy which showed that the vigor of his youth had not departed from him.

Four or five of the young men began to dance, posturing in different attitudes, moving their arms and legs, stamping on the floor, all in perfect accord with one another, and keeping accurate time with the drum. We were too tired, however, to appreciate this exhibition, and signified as much to the company, who finally left us to enjoy a good night's rest.

TUESDAY, 9TH. — WE were awakened by an officious native, who put his head in, bawling at the top of his lungs that the weather was bad, very bad indeed, and that we could not get away today; after which pleasing piece of information he left us to our own reflections.

On getting up and going out I found that the sky was cloudy and the wind adverse, and ordering one of our Máhlemuts to put on the chynik, I went down and reported the situation, which involved our remaining a day or two where we were. Breakfast, consisting of chy, with sugar,—but of course no milk,—biscuit, and a savory piece of bacon, was duly discussed; and after a comforting pipe, we were quite ready to bear our detention with the true voyageur's philosophy.

I went out, and soon made the acquaintance, by signs and the very few native words which I had picked up, of a fine-looking young Máhlemut, who was also on his way to Unalaklík with his family. The interview commenced by his begging for a little tobacco, upon receiving which he was so delighted as to take me to his tent, a poor little affair, made of unbleached sheeting procured from the Russians. Here he introduced me by signs to his wife and child, the latter about two years old. The former was not particularly ugly or pretty, but was engaged in manufacturing tinder, which rather detracted from the neatness of her person. This tinder is made out of the fur of the rabbit, the down from the seed-vessels of the river poplar, or cotton link obtained from the Russians; either of which is rubbed up with charcoal and water, with a very little gunpowder, and then dried. The rubbing process was just going on, and I was thankful that etiquette did not require hand-shaking, among the Innuit of Norton Sound. The husband was a fine-looking, athletic fellow, standing about five feet five inches, with a clear brunette complexion, fine color, dark eyes, and finely arched eyebrows. The flat nose, common to all the Eskimo tribes, was not very strongly marked in him, and a pleasant smile displaying two rows of very white teeth conquered any objection I might have felt to his large mouth. The baby looked like any other baby, and was notable only from never showing any disposition to disturb the peace.

Returning after a while to the casine, I observed that the aperture in the roof was closed by a covering composed of the intestines of seals, cut down on one side, cleaned, oiled, and sewed together into a sheet, which is sufficiently translucent to admit the light while it retains the warm air.

The universal salutation of the Innuit is *Chammi! Chammi!* and as likely as not, some greasy old fellow will hug you like a brother upon a first meeting. As they are given to raising a certain kind of live-stock, this method of proceeding is not likely to suit the fastidious.

A note arrived from Westdahl by a native, one of his crew, saying that on account of rough weather he had been obliged to put into a small cove, some miles south of us, had cut his bidarrá on the rocks and wet almost everything.

Ketchum immediately despatched four men with a needle, some twisted thread made of deer sinew, called *gíla*, and a piece of sealskin prepared for use, technically known as *luvták*. These, with some grease to rub on the seam, are all that is needed to repair any injury done to the skin of a bidarrá or bidárka.

FRIDAY, 12TH. — ROSE with the determination of going somewhere where there were no *terrankánoff*, as the Russians call the insects with which their apartment was infested. I obtained a tent, pitched it, and moved most of my traps out into it. Planted a flag-pole and threw the ensign of the Scientific Corps to the breeze, with the resolution to carry the blue cross and scallop, before the year was out, where no other flat had yet floated, if that were possible.

I began to provide myself with suitable clothing, such as the natives wear. First, an *artégi*, or *párka*, as the Russians call it. This is a shirt of dressed deerskin, with the hair on, coming down to the knees, and to be confined by a belt around the waist. There is no opening in the breast or back, but a hood large enough to cover the head, which may be pushed back when not needed. This garment is trimmed around the skirt, wrists, and hood with strips of white deerskin and wolverine or wolf-skin, both of which are highly prized for the purpose. Around the hood the wolfskin is broad and taken from the back of the animal, where the longest hairs are barred with white and black, which, when the hood is drawn up, makes a kind of halo about the face which is not unbecoming. When travelling, these long hairs shield the face from a side wind to a surprising extent. The parka is exceedingly warm, and the wind does not penetrate it; while in exceedingly cold weather a light one, made of fawn-skin, or *wiperotky*, as the Russians term it, may be worn with the hair turned in, inside of the usual garment, which is made of various skins, according to the fancy. The fall skin of the young deer, known as *neédress*, is the most common and perhaps the best. The skins of Parry's marmot (*Spermophilus Parryi*) and the muskrat (*Fiber zibethicus*) are praised for their durability, and wiperotky parkies are neat and light, but do not last long. On the whole the needress is as strong, durable, and warm as any, and almost as handsome when well trimmed.

The next most important articles are the *torbassá* or Eskimo boots. These are made of the skin of the reindeer's legs, where the hair is short, smooth, and stiff. These are sewed together to make the tops of the boots, which come up nearly to the knee, where they are tied. The sole is made of sealskin, or luvták prepared in the same way as for making boats. This sole is turned over at heel and toe, and gathered like the skirt of a dress, so as to protect those parts, and brought up on each side. It is of course nearly waterproof and rather durable, but can be easily replaced in half an hour by a new one if necessary. It is wetted before being sewed, which makes the sealskin flexible, and the proper formation of the toe is aided by the teeth of the seamstress. In wearing these boots, which are made much larger than the foot, a pad of dry grass, folded to the shape of the sole, is worn under the foot. This absorbs any moisture, serves as a non-conductor, and protects the foot from the inequalities of ice or the soil. The whole furnishes a warm and comfortable covering, indispensable to winter travel. There are a pair of strings, one on each side, which are tied about the ankle, supporting it and preventing the foot from slipping about in the boot.

Deerskin breeches are worn by the natives, but are rarely needed by white men when provided with clothing of ordinary warmth and thickness.

The value of a good parka is at present about six dollars. Boots and other articles are usually obtained by barter. Ten musket-balls and a few caps are the regular price for a pair of torbassá, a pair of deerskin mittens being worth from four to six balls; ornamental gloves and other articles are more or less costly, according to the amount of work and the scarcity of the article at the time. So far, the natives have not yet learned to make a well-shaped thumb to gloves and mittens, a triangular shapeless protuberance serving their needs, but they may be easily taught a better mode of manufacture.

A deer or bear skin in the raw, dry state is used as a bed, and a blanket of dressed deer or rabbit skins, in addition to a pair of woollen ones, completes the list of articles needed for winter travel, though a small pillow is a great addition to one's comfort. A deerskin is worth, at the regular price, about sixty cents.

MONDAY, 29TH. — AFTER a long night's rest, woke a good deal refreshed, though rather stiff, and enjoyed our breakfast thoroughly. Francis and myself took a walk some distance up the river, finding many open places in the ice. After our return I made a few sketches of the houses and Indians and obtained a beginning of a vocabulary of Ingalik words. These Indians all understand a little Russian, and by this means are enabled to communicate with the whites. No one in the territory understands any English. The Innuit, especially the Máhlemut dialect, is so easy to acquire that the fur-traders learn it in preference to attempting the difficult task of teaching them Russian. Very few of the Innuit understand any Russian, while almost all the Russians understand some Eskimo. On the other hand, the Indian dialect is so much harder to learn than the Russian, that the Indians pick up Russian with facility, while none of the Russians, except an old interpreter named Teléezhik, know more than a few words of the Indian dialects.

In the afternoon Ingechuk brought us some white grouse and some fresh reindeer meat. Of the latter a delicious dish was concocted, which I will describe for the benefit of future explorers. It was invented by the members of Kennicott's party during the first year's exploration. The frozen reindeer meat was cut into small cubes about half an inch in diameter. An equal amount of backfat was treated in the same way. Hardly covered with water, this was simmered in a stewpan for nearly an hour; water, pepper, and salt being added as needed. When nearly done, a little more water was added, and the finely broken biscuit from the bottom of the bread-bag slowly stirred in, until the whole of the gravy was absorbed. This done, we sat down to enjoy a dish which would have awakened enthusiasm at the table of Lucullus. It was known among the initiated as "telegraph stew," and the mere mention of its name would no doubt touch, in the breast of any of them, a chord of electric sympathy.

The Russian name for the reindeer is *alêné*, perhaps derived from the French. These deer are migratory, feeding on the twigs of the willow and the fine white moss, or rather lichen, which is to be found on every hillside. They frequent the hills during the summer, and are driven thence only by the mosquitoes to seek refuge in the water. In the fall and winter they prefer the more sheltered valleys, and appear on the plains in immense herds in the spring.

TUESDAY, 30TH. — WALKED down the river, and, looking into some deserted Indian huts, obtained some exquisite green mosses and lichens which were flourishing there notwithstanding the cold weather.

A number of sleds arrived from Unalaklík, bringing a large amount of goods and provisions for transmission to Nuláto.

On the rolling plain between the summer houses and the bases of the Ulûkuk Hills I found the larch (*Larix microcarpa?*) growing sparingly to the height of twelve feet, and abundance of alders. The snow-covered sides of these symmetrical hills stood out with striking beauty against the dark clouds which formed the background of a rich crimson and purple sunset.

SUNDAY, 4TH. — IN the morning a strong northeast wind was blowing, with the thermometer about 16°, and a great deal of loose snow driving about. I determined, in spite of the remonstrances of the others, to delay no longer, and, putting some biscuit and ukali in my pocket, I started alone, about eleven o'clock, for Iktígalik. The wind sweeping over the broad plains near the mouth of the river was so violent, and the sleet was so blinding, that I was unable to face it, and was obliged to go from side to side of the river diagonally. In doing this I was misled by a branch of the river, and proceeded several miles before I found out my mistake. Retracing my steps, I took the right direction, and reached the wooded part of the river, where the trees made a shelter from the force of the wind and driving snow, late in the afternoon. I found the ice rather soft and covered in many places with drifted snow, so that the travelling was very laborious. To add to my annoyances, it soon became very dark, and I had to grope my way over ice-hummocks and through snow-drifts until nearly worn out by the exertion. Passing round a bend in the river, the ice gave way under me, and I had only time to throw myself on one side, where it proved more solid, and I got off with a wetting up to my knees. Taking off my boots and socks, I wrung out the water and put them on again, when they froze immediately. Nothing but the want of an axe prevented my camping then and there; but a howling, which came evidently from no great distance, reminded me that it might not prove healthy to sleep without a fire. I trudge along, and, to my great delight, about eight o'clock, the moon rose, and I soon saw the high caches of the village standing out against the sky. I heard no dogs, however, and on reaching the entrance of the house on the bank I found it closed with a block of wood. Climbing on to the roof and looking through the gut cover, I thought I saw a glimmer as of live coals where the fire had been. My shouts finally aroused Ingechuk, who was the only occupant. Ketchum had evidently gone, and I had my labor for my pains! Between the small stock of Russian which I had picked up, and the little Ingechuk knew, I finally managed to make out that they had left that day and gone to Ulúkuk. I made him boil the chynik, and changed my wet clothes, which were frozen so hard as to be difficult to get off; and then, after taking my tea, retired with a feeling that I had earned a good night's sleep.

FRIDAY, 23D. — ROSE early, and after reloading the sleds and discussing chy, with accompaniments of bacon, biscuit, ukali, and molasses, we passed on over hillsides sparsely wooded with spruce and alder, through valleys, and up and down some rather bad hills, occasionally along the river on the ice. About dark we came upon some open tundra, just beyond a low marsh, known as Beaver Lake, as it is covered with water in the spring; here a strong north wind was blowing full in our teeth, carrying the snow along the ground in blinding sleet. The atmosphere was six below zero. The other sleds were some distance behind, but as our sled carried the teakettle and axes, we felt pretty sure the Indians would follow, though much against their will. We struggled on until we arrived at an old camp of Ketchum's, where one tree mocked us with its inefficient attempt at shelter. We decided to camp here, no more suitable locality being within reach. By placing the sleds to windward, with a piece of cotton drill stretched around them, we managed to keep off the driving snow a little. The hot tea in our tin cups burned the hand on one side, while the keen wind gnawed it on the other. Smoking was out of the question, and we lay down, using the bacon as pillows, and watched the dogs, who, growling their disapprobation, sheltered their noses with their tails, and, more fortunate than ourselves, soon sank into unconscious slumber.

SATURDAY, 24TH. — ABOUT four o'clock in the morning an old Indian called Iván, from Nuláto, came along with his son. They pulled their own sled, and had a few marten skins with which they were going to Unalaklík to buy oil for winter use. Shortly after, we broke camp and proceeded. About nine o'clock the sun rose, attended by three beautiful mock suns, or *parhelia*. One was nearly thirty degrees above the real sun, and there was one on each side, similar, but more brilliant. All were connected by an arch resembling a rainbow, except that it was of an orange color with a dark reddish bank on the inner side, and threw out rays of light from the outer edge. About a quarter of another similar arch was reversed, touching the lower arch at the point where the upper mock sun was seen, and a cross of brilliant light was noticed at each junction of the arch between the mock suns. This beautiful exhibition continued for six hours, from sunrise to sunset, and Mike tells me they are not uncommon here in winter.

Shot a Canada jay, or whiskey jack (*Perisoreus canadenis*), with a dark brown "woolly bear" caterpillar in his mouth, just killed. Where it had come from was a mystery I do not pretend to solve, probably from beneath the snow.

We decided to camp early, as we were all very tired, and after descending a deep declivity called by the Russians *Perivǎlli*, we stopped on the bank of a small stream, made a good camp, enjoyed our supper, tea, and pipes, and slept soundly.

SUNDAY, 26TH. — OFF at six. Passed over the flanks of some high hills, from one of which I caught my first glimpse of the great river Yúkon, broad, smooth, and ice-bound. A natural impatience urged me forward, and after a smart tramp of several miles we arrived at the steep bank of the river. It was with a feeling akin to that which urged Balboa forward into the very waves of a newly discovered ocean, that I rushed by the dogs and down the steep declivity, forgetting everything else in the desire to be the first on the ice, and to enjoy the magnificent prospect before me.

There lay a stretch of forty miles of this great, broad, snow-covered river, with broken fragments of ice-cakes glowing in the ruddy light of the setting sun; the low opposite shore, three miles away, seemed a mere black streak on the horizon. A few islands covered with dark evergreens were in sight above. Below, a faint purple tinged the snowy crests of far-off mountains, whose height, though not extreme, seemed greater from the low banks near me and the clear sky beyond. This was the river I had read and dreamed of, which had seemed as if shrouded in mystery, in spite of the tales of those who had seen it. On its banks lived thousands who know neither its outlet nor its source, who look to it for food and even for clothing, and, recognizing its magnificence, call themselves proudly *men of the Yukon.*

Stolid indeed must he be, who surveys the broad expanse of the Missouri of the North for the first time without emotion. A little Innuit lad, who ran before the dogs and saw it for the first time, shouted at the sight, saying, amidst his expressions of astonishment, "It is not a river, it is a sea!" and even the Indians had no word of ridicule for him, often as they had seen it.

DANA STABENOW

Dead in the Water

AFTER EXTENSIVE RESEARCH and careful study of the resulting
data, the National Oceanic and Atmospheric Administration has decreed
that on average there are only eight days of sunshine per year in the
Aleutian Islands. This day, midway through October, usually the first
month of the storm season, was, incredibly, one of them. The storm that
had blown the *Avilda* back to Dutch had blown out again, and on its heels
was a high pressure system that stretched as high, wide and handsome as
they could see in every direction. The view from five thousand feet up
was spectacular.

"I don't believe this," Kate said over her headset.

"Don't believe what?" Jack said. He barely cradled the yoke in one

---

*Alaskan native Dana Stabenow is the author of a string of Kate Shugak
mysteries, including* A Cold Day for Murder *and* A Fatal Thaw. *1993's*
Dead in the Water *is the latest thriller.*

large fist, his feet relaxed on the pedals. There was no turbulence, and Cecily the Cessna sailed smoothly down the Aleutian sky for all the world like a Cadillac sailing down a freshly paved section of interstate.

"I don't believe that, for one thing," she said, pointing to Jack's relaxed grip. "I don't believe you're steering this crate with one finger."

His look was of mild surprise. "Why not?"

"This is *October*," she replied. "This is the *Aleutians*. This kind of weather doesn't happen in October in the Aleutians. From what I've heard and read, this kind of weather hardly ever happens here at all, during any time of the year. You should hear fishermen talking about the Aleutians when they're back home. The winds alone, the williwaws—they call this place the Cradle of the Winds, did you know that? All my life, listening to those guys' stories, I've thought this place was some kind of hellhole. But look at it," she said with a sweep of her hand, her tone caught between astonishment and awe. "Just look at it."

The islands strung out before them, as far as they could see, in a long, slow, southwesterly curve. The white peaks glowed against the deep blue of the sea, like a string of pearls draped across a shell of blue-tinted mother-of-pearl in a jeweler's window. Each island had its own volcano, rising steeply to tickle at the belly of the sky, and most of them were smoking or steaming or both. The cones were smoothed over with termination dust, which began near the summit of each mountain in a heavy layer of frozen icing, thinning out to a scant layer of vanilla frosting nearer the shoreline. The snow did not so much soften the islands' rugged outlines as it emphasized them. Beneath it, in dramatic shifts of shadow and sunlight, every island was a rough and tumble surge of magmatic rock, thrust violently up from the bowels of mother earth straight down into the sea. In those topographical entrails could be read the history of the planet.

"It's like watching the earth being born," Kate said softly. "I've never seen anything like it."

Jack looked as satisfied as if he'd arranged for the Aleutians to be where they were, the day to be as clear as it was, and for the *Avilda* to break down just when it did, all to get Kate in the air at this place, at this time, in his company. For the next two hours they forgot they were on their way to the scene of the mysterious disappearance of two ship's crewmen, and played at sight-seeing and rubbernecking in the best tradition of the American tourist. They flew low over a brief stretch of sand littered with the green glass balls Japanese fishermen use for net floats. They annoyed a herd of walrus sunbathing on another beach, until a bull in the crowd, a magnificent old beast with tusks two feet long, reared up and roared at them, daring them to come on down. Off the shore of still another island they found a stand of sea stacks, weird towers of rock sculpted by sand and wind and engulfed in flocks of gulls and cormorants, and as they banked for another look, Kate saw three bald eagles take wing. Hot springs steamed up from cupped valleys, the tall Aleutian rye grass clustering thick and still green around them.

Kate had a nagging feeling something was wrong, and took a moment to identify it. "No trees!"

"What?"

"There aren't any trees!"

Jack looked over at her with a raised eyebrow. "Even I know there aren't any trees in the Aleutians, Kate. And even I know why. The wind blows too hard."

"I know, I know, I just—I'd forgotten."

"There are trees in Unalaska, though." He nodded at her look of incredulity. "But they were brought there. I was talking to a guy yesterday. There's a stand of firs, planted by the Russians almost two hundred years ago. And it appears they are just now beginning to reproduce."

He looked at her, waiting, and she said approvingly, "Very good, Jack. Where'd you stumble across all this local color?"

"Wasn't a hell of a lot to do in Dutch Harbor, waiting for your boat to come in. I'd been sleeping in the back"—he jerked a thumb toward the back of the plane—"and she was parked off to one side of the strip, and you know how people who work around planes are. I shot the breeze with whoever felt like talking. Interesting place. Dutch, not the airstrip."

"I haven't had a chance to sightsee myself, yet. Maybe next time in, if we have any time on shore."

"With any luck, we'll find out what happened to those two yo-yos and you won't have to go out again." He peered through the wind-shield, squinting against the sun, and consulted a map unfolded on his lap. "That should be Anua, dead ahead."

Kate craned her neck for the first look at the little island. It had two mountains, one three thousand feet high and smoking, the other half its height and serene beneath a layer of snow. Between the two lay a valley, its surface barely above sea level, narrow and as flat as an ironing board. "I can see why they put a base there during the war," Kate observed.

"It's a natural site," Jack agreed, "and the island is right on the air route between Dutch and Adak. Good place for an emergency landing. Look, over there, south side of the island, west side of the beach. Yeah. That's where Gault says the two guys went ashore." He put the plane into a steep dive and they flew up and then down the long, curving beach.

"There's the strip," Kate said, pointing inland.

"So it is, and it looks in fair shape, too." All the same, Jack flew down the runway three times, gear five feet off the deck, checking for rocks and bumps and holes. When he was satisfied he circled again, lowered the flaps and sideslipped down to a perfect three-point landing.

Kate hid a smile and said mildly, "Show-off." If possible, Jack's expression became even more smug, and she added, "Too bad you can't do that at Merrill Field in Anchorage."

He laughed. "Too many people there. I can only do it right when nobody's watching." He cut the engine and in the sudden silence added, "This strip's in good shape. Not much snow, but what there is, is packed down. No big ruts, either. Curious. For an abandoned strip."

"Maybe hunters use it."

He shook his head. "Fishermen, maybe. Island's too small to support anything worth packing out."

The Cessna had rolled out to a stop twenty feet from a tumbledown assortment of shacks, most of them minus their roof and some missing a wall or two. Kicking through the debris, they found nothing of interest beyond a tattered, water-soaked cover of *Life* magazine featuring Betty Grable's legs, and a half-buried metal tank with a pump handle mounted on the outside. Jack tried the pump and to their surprise it worked smoothly. A few cranks and fluid gushed out of the spout, to melt and puddle in the snow on the ground. The smell of gasoline struck sharply at their nostrils.

"Av gas," Jack said.

"How do you know?"

"It's green," he said, pointing to the puddle beneath the spout. "Aviation gas is green. Plain old gas gas, like you put in the car, is clear."

"Oh. Right." Kate stared at the widening puddle, her eyebrows drawing together.

"Besides," Jack was saying, "what else kind of gas would you expect to find right next to an airstrip? I wonder how long it's been sitting here? Twenty, thirty years, you think? Might have been here since the war." Catching sight of her puzzled expression, he said, "What?"

"I don't know," she said slowly, still staring at the puddle of green gas. "There's something about av gas I remember from when I was a kid, but . . ." She shook her head and smiled at him. "At two o'clock this morning I'll probably sit bolt upright in bed and shout it out."

"Not if you're in the sack with me, you won't," he told her.

"Whatever you say." She grinned at him. "Come on. Let's walk down to the beach."

It was Jack who found it, or rather fell through the roof of it. He'd been wandering behind her, through the tall rye grass poking up through the thin layer of crusted snow, enjoying the sun and the salt breeze and the sound of the surf, when the previously solid ground beneath his feet gave way and suddenly he was sliding through the turf and into an empty space beneath.

"Hey," he said. The turf engulfed his legs and started up his butt to nibble at his waist and he raised his voice. "Hey? Hey! Hey, Kate! Kate! Help! *Help!*"

He kicked out with his legs, trying to find purchase, something to brace himself against, and immediately slid in up to his chest. His hands scrabbled around and grasped at the grass, anything to keep him from sliding even farther into what his naturally strong sense of optimism assured him was probably a bubbling pit of volcanic lava. If it came to that, he suffered from a lifelong case of acrophobia, and would have preferred a pit of lava to an empty, endless abyss.

Kate's head appeared, ending this morbid speculation, and peered down at him through the rye grass with interest. "What seems to be the problem?"

"What the hell does it look like, I'm falling into the center of the earth here! Get me out!"

She looked at him, pursing her lips, displaying less concern than he considered the situation warranted. "I wonder—" Abruptly, her head vanished again from sight.

He panicked, just a little, no more than he considered absolutely necessary. "Wait! Where the hell you going? Kate!"

"Relax," he heard her say. He waited, unrelaxed, sweating beneath his jacket and clutching at some very insubstantial stalks of grass. An over-active imagination conjured up a chasm beneath his dangling legs, a bottom-less chasm into which he would fall and keep falling—

Something grabbed hold of his right foot and gave a vigorous tug. "Hey!" he yelled.

"Relax," Kate said again, laughter in her voice, which seemed now to be coming from beneath him. "It's only me. The floor's about two feet beneath you. Let go and slide on down."

He hesitated. "Are you sure?"

"Would I lie to you?"

Her voice sounded entirely too innocent to suit him, but he trusted her enough to let go of the grass, one stalk at a time. Nothing happened. He raised his arms and wriggled a little. His shoulders caught in the hole for a moment, before the edges of the hole disintegrated and he slipped through in a rain of soil and grass.

Almost at once his feet hit solid ground. Staggering, he caught his balance and found himself in a small room, square, twelve feet on a side. The walls had been dug into the surface of the island and, looking up, through the dim light coming through the hole he'd made he could see that the builders had roofed the room over in turf and let the grass do the rest.

"People have been here," Kate said positively, standing next to him.

"Well, of course people have been here, Kate, even I can tell that this is a man-made structure."

"No, I mean recently," she told him. He followed her pointing finger and saw a half-dozen cases of Van Camp's Pork and Beans stacked next to a virtual tower of Costco's twenty-four-roll packages of ScotTissue Premium two-ply Bathroom Tissue.

He walked over to take a closer look. "All the essentials of life." He raised his head and stared around. "The Coasties never said anything about this place. I don't remember reading about it in any of the reports on the search missions. They must have missed it completely."

"I don't know," Kate said, "all you have to do is fall through the roof."

Jack ignored her. "Alcala and Brown must have missed it, too. Too bad. They could have holed up here for days." One of the boxes was open, and grinning a little, he pulled out a can and held it up. "Dinner might have gotten a little monotonous, but hell." The can slipped and he almost dropped it. Something cool and gooey ran over his fingers. "What the hell?"

Even with the new skylight in the roof there wasn't enough light in the little room to see what he was talking about. "What's wrong?" she said, peering into the dim corner in which he was standing.

A booted foot crunched on sand, and she recoiled when a disembodied hand thrust a can of pork and beans in her face. "Yuk," she said, wrinkling her nose at the smell. "Somebody leave the rest of his supper behind?"

"I don't think so." Brushing by her, Jack stooped to go through the door. His voice was grim, and Kate followed him outside.

The light confirmed what his fingertips had felt. The can was punctured, a hole the size of a .38 caliber bullet entering the V in Van and exiting just above the bottom seam.

Jack regarded the hole meditatively. "Think whoever put this stuff here used it for target practice?"

Without answering, Kate ducked back inside the dugout. Together they hauled out everything inside. As they removed each box, Jack marked it with his omnipresent black Marksalot, and they restacked them outside in the same position they had been in inside. The contents of the perforated cans had spilled out over the cases and dried to a sticky dark brown that looked like old blood. "Some of it might be old blood," Jack observed. The outward facing surface common to three of the boxes, the three messiest ones, looked crumpled, as if a heavy weight had slammed into them where they were stacked against the dugout's wall.

Jack stood looking at the cardboard boxes, hands in his pockets. "What we got here is two choices," he said at last.

"And they are?"

"Either somebody was really and I mean *really* tired of pork and beans."

"Or?" Their eyes met. Her mouth compressed into a thin line. "You got a can opener in the plane?"

They opened every case and then every can with a hole in it. They found a dozen such cans and, rattling around in the sixth box they opened, one long slug. Jack held up the misshapen piece of metal and said, "This could be anything from a .22 to a .357." Nevertheless, he stored it carefully away in a Ziploc bag. Into another Ziploc he scraped some of the dried brown fluid from the front of one of the boxes. He'd brought a flashlight back with the can opener and they examined the floor of the dugout, without result. Jack bagged some samples of the dirt anyway. He made several drawings of the scene, and when he was through they repacked the cans in their cases and loaded them into the back of the Cessna. The toilet paper, which had survived the armed assault relatively unscathed— "Naturally," Jack said, "the slug would have been in a lot better shape if it had impacted the asswipe"—was stacked back where they'd found it.

The little room, dark and dank and smelling of mildew, had begun to close in around Kate and she was glad to leave it. The air outside felt fresh and clean and she pulled it into her lungs in big, cleansing breaths.

The dugout stood on the south slope of a tiny rise that fell away to the beach. Jack stood with his back to the water, looking at the structure, impressed by its air of having grown there. The rye grass grew tall and thick and right up to the walls and over the roof, and even now, in winter, from three, even two steps away, the door was invisible. He could see how the Coasties had missed it. Of course, they hadn't been looking with murder in mind. "Who built this place? And why?"

"You said this island has a natural strategic location," Kate reminded him, pulling the door closed, noting as she did that it was made of meticulously assembled planks in which no nail had been placed without careful thought and attention. "You think the Aleuts wouldn't have noticed that, too?"

He was skeptical. "You think there was a village here at one time? You think this place has been here that long?"

"Why not? It's built in the old way. Those dirt walls have been there so long they feel like concrete. Look at this door. Those planks are salvage, and old salvage at that. See? Hand-planed. And these nails? Those weren't mass-produced. Some whaler broke up offshore a hundred years ago and whoever lived here made doors out of the wreck. And that whole you fell through."

"What about it?"

"Before the Russians introduced doors, the Aleuts built these *barabaras* with the doors in the roof." She looked around. "I bet if we looked, we'd find the ruins of others."

"There are no records of a village on Anua, Kate. There's no mark on the map for archaeological ruins. This is probably just some seal hunter's cabin."

She shook her head. "The beach is long, wide and relatively level. There aren't that many good beaches in the Aleutians. Mostly it's just one steep slide from mountaintop to ocean bottom. That makes this a natural site"—she gave him a brief smile—"for landing kayaks."

They walked the ten feet to where the rye grass left off and the beach began. Over a mile in length, Kate estimated, with a jumbled rock formation on one end and cliffs on the other. A creek burbled seaward, cutting a shallow bed through the center of the beach down to the water-line. There, the surf pounded viciously at the gravel, and the ebb and flow of the swells coming in from the southeast alternately revealed and swallowed up a half-dozen reefs within the curve of the land, staggered one after the other, jagged and threatening. "Yeah," Jack said dryly, "real inviting place to beach a boat."

"They would have found a way in," Kate said, positive. "And it would have been a tremendous natural defense against attack."

"What are you looking at?"

Her eyes were squinted against the sun. "Right there, I—yes! I think it is!" she cried, pointing, and took off running.

"Oh, Christ," Jack said, and took off after her.

He caught up with her where the towers of rock broke the furious surf into white sheets of spray some hundred feet away. Not near far enough away, in his humble opinion, and he was about to say so when he saw that she was stripping out of her clothes. His heartbeat, which had started to slow down at no sign of a mad marksman with a mad on for Van Camp's Pork and Beans, began once again to speed up. "What in the hell are you doing, Shugak?"

"Look," she said, pointing in front of them.

"What?" He cast about wildly for some reason for Kate to be stripping down to the buff, on an Aleutian Island, between the Gulf of Alaska and the Bering Sea, in the middle of October.

They were standing at the edge of a tumble of rock that stretched between beach and the rock towers. The surf pounded at the towers in what Jack considered to be determined and ominous fashion. Some amphibious mammal, probably one with very large and very sharp teeth, was barking in large numbers somewhere beyond those rock towers. Gulls screamed and dived in the blue sky above. Kate gave an exasperated sigh at his confused expression and pointed again. "Right in front of you, idiot."

His gaze dropped. Directly in front of the toes of his boots, on the tumble of rocks between them and the ominous surf, there was a series of shallow pools in the dips and hollows between the rocks. One of the larger pools began at their feet, stretched out some twelve feet across and looked to be some three to four feet deep. He gave the still, green surface a suspicious look. "Tidal pools?" he said. "So what?"

"Not tidal pools, hot springs!" Kate said impatiently. "See the steam! Can't you smell the sulfur?" She shucked out of panties and bra and waded in. "I knew it!" she said, feeling her way with her feet. "The bottom is almost smooth and—yes," she said, bending over and feeling beneath the surface with her hands, "I can feel where they leveled out a place to sit." She turned and lowered herself into the water. It came up almost to her chin, and she let loose with a long, voluptuous sigh. "Not too hot, not too cold, just exactly, perfectly right."

Her spirits rose with her body temperature, and the ghosts she had felt pressing about her as she worked in the dugout dissolved in the wisps of steam that rose from the water's surface. She looked at Jack, one corner of her mouth curling. The challenge was implicit. He gritted his teeth and bent over to unlace his boots. She watched with enjoyment, and went so far as to hum the tune to "The Stripper" when he got to his belt. He had a terrible time with the buttons of his jeans.

When he lowered himself into the water next to her Jack was amazed to discover that this wasn't some perfidious Shugak practical joke after all. The water was hot, but not too hot. It bubbled up around him in a natural Jacuzzi and sizzled right through his skin into his bones. "Oh, yeah," he said, relaxing with a long, satisfied groan. Curious, he tasted the water. "It's not very salty," he said in surprise.

"It's probably a mixture," she said, leaning back and closing her eyes. "Salt from the spray, fresh from underground."

He looked over and admired the way her body shone up at him through the water. It was a perfect body in his eyes, compact, well muscled, just the right balance of lean to soft, lithe in motion and at rest. Her face was broad across the cheekbones, softening to a small, stubborn chin that held up a wide, determined mouth. Her hazel eyes tilted up at the sides with the hint of an epicanthic fold. Even the twisted scar that stretched across her throat almost from ear to ear looked right today, a badge of honor, an emblem of courage. A warning, too. Anyone who had a scar like that and was still around to wear it was not someone you wanted to mess with.

She opened her eyes and caught him admiring, and after that they didn't talk for a while.

"Nice day," Jack said, in an inadequate expression of postcoital bliss.

"Enjoy it," Kate replied, her face nuzzled into his neck. "It'll get worse."

The lover in him didn't move a muscle. The pilot looked nervously over her head to the southeast for signs of an incoming weather front, and found only the merest wisps of cloud low on the horizon. "How do you know?"

"Because in the Aleutians the one rule is, if the weather is good, it'll get bad. And if it's bad, it'll get worse. During the war, the air force lost two times the amount of casualties and five times the amount of planes to weather and mechanical trouble due to weather than they did in combat." She mustered up enough energy to point. "See the end of the runway?"

He didn't bother to turn his head. "Sure."

"You're lucky. It was more than the World War II pilots could see. They didn't have radar at first and the weather'd be so bad the pilot waiting for takeoff would have to radio to the guy taking off in front of him to find out if he'd left the ground or not, before he could make his try." She raised her head and looked at him. "And then, once they were in the air, assuming of course they did make it into the air, they were flying on naval charts based on a Russian survey made in 1864. Assuming of course they could see anything once they got into the air."

"Sounds like fun to me." He rubbed the small of her back, surveying the treeless expanse of bog and rock, and the heaving, swelling sea stretching endlessly beyond. "Why'd they bother?"

"They had to. If the Japanese took Alaska, they'd have been within bombing range of Boeing. Not to mention Russia. There's only fifty-seven miles of water between the Alaskan and Russian coasts. It was a major Lend-Lease route, through Fairbanks and Nome." She added, "Plus, the Japanese lost at Midway because they were attacking Dutch Harbor at the same time. It split their forces at a time when they were infinitely superior to us in the Pacific."

"Divide and conquer."

"Something like that."

"You know a lot about it."

"There's a book, a good one, on the war in the Aleutians, written by a guy named Garfield. And . . ."

"And what?"

"And," Kate said, a little embarrassed to discover she was proud of it, "my father was one of Castner's Cutthroats."

Jack looked blank. "One of what?"

"Castner's Cutthroats. Also known as the Alaska Scouts."

He drew back and looked down at her questioningly. "Don't stop there. Were they some sort of troops, or what?"

Kate grinned. "More 'or what,' if you could believe my father. They were kind of like Special Forces, long on fighting ability and short on discipline, but you could expect that from the kind of men they were. Castner must have hit every bar in the bush signing them up. Dad said there were prospectors, homesteaders, doctors, hunters, trappers, fishermen. I think they even bagged an anthropologist or two, probably out of the University of Alaska."

"They see any action?"

"They went ashore at Attu before the regular troops. It was in-your-face fighting every step of the way. There was even a banzai charge with bayonets, near the end, when the Japanese knew they were beat." Kate shivered. "Messy. Oh, yeah, Dad could strip his sleeves and show his scars with the best of them."

"Shock troops."

"I guess." Kate looked around again. "I wonder what happened to them."

"Who, Castner's Cutthroats?"

"No. The Anuans."

The rock seat beneath him having been worn indisputably smooth by generations of buttocks before he had taken up residence, Jack was no longer disposed to argue over the existence of an Aleut settlement on Anua. "Maybe they were moved out during the war."

"You said there was no record of a settlement on Anua," she reminded him.

"Oh, yeah. Right." He thought. "Didn't I just read something in the papers about how Congress passed an act to compensate the Aleutian Aleuts for being uprooted from their homes during World War II?"

Kate nodded. "Yeah. In 1989. The survivors got sixteen bucks for every day they spent in the camps."

"What did happen, back then? I never have heard the full story."

Kate's shoulders moved in a faint shrug. "It was war, the Japanese had attacked Pearl Harbor and invaded Attu and Kiska. The military authorities could pretty much do as they liked, so they bundled up every last Aleut from the Rat Islands north and settled them in villages in south-central Alaska. After the war, almost none of them were resettled in their original villages, and the soldiers trashed what little housing was left standing. They'd burned or bulldozed most of it anyway, either to keep the Japs from using it or to make way for their own construction."

"But it was war," Jack pointed out.

"I know."

"If things had gone the other way, they could have wound up prisoners of the Japanese."

"Some of them did. Some Aleuts the Japanese took prisoner off Attu and Kiska. In Japan, they put them to work, and even paid them for it." Kate smiled. "When they were repatriated, their biggest difficulty was in getting their Japanese paychecks cashed."

"How come you know so much about this?"

A muscle cramped in her thigh and she grunted and shifted off him. He whimpered a little in protest but didn't stop her. "Jack, I'm an Aleut." She waited for that to register, but he looked blank. "I'm an Aleut living in an area historically inhabited by Athapascans, Eyaks, and

Tlingits." His blank expression began to change to comprehension, and she nodded. "My family comes from around here somewhere. We were expatriated along with the rest of the Aleuts. We had relatives in Cordova, so we moved to the Park."

"No wonder you took this job."

She ducked her head, embarrassed again, this time to be discovered in a moment of racial sentimentality. "Yeah. I guess I just wanted to see what the old home place looked like." She squinted up at the sun and added, "We'd better get a move on if we want to make it back to Dutch before dark."

"I've got a tarp in the back of the plane," he said, reaching for his pants.

"So?"

"So, we can tack it over that hole I made in the roof of the dugout."

"*Barabara.*"

"Whatever."

Her smile was reward enough for the thought, and realizing it, he knew he had it bad. In the air the following morning, when he banked the Cessna for a last look at the honeymoon suite in the hot springs, he was sure of it.

As they climbed another thousand feet, over the sound of the engine Kate said, "You think somebody got shot in the *barabara?*"

"Yup."

"Maybe somebody who was hiding out from somebody else?"

"Yup."

Kate was unable to keep herself from wondering which one. Alcala or Brown. The sexy ascetic or the teddy bear. Whose dried and darkened blood had it been that had spilled over the cardboard cases, had mingled with the gravy oozing from the broken cans and dripped down, to lose all color and identity until it became one with the dirt floor?

Could have been both, she realized. No reason why not. The mental picture of the two young men, spending the remaining minutes of their lives cowering between the cases of pork and beans and the rolls of toilet paper, was enough to keep her silent all the way back to Dutch.

JACK LONDON

An Odyssey of the North

"I WILL TALK of the things which were, in my own way; but you will understand. I will begin at the beginning, and tell of myself and the woman, and, after that, of the man."

He of the Otter Skins drew over to the stove as do men who have been deprived of fire and are afraid the Promethean gift may vanish at any moment. Malemute Kid pricked up the slush-lamp, and placed it so its light fell upon the face of the narrator. Prince slid his body over the edge of the bunk and joined them.

"I am Naass, a chief, and the son of a chief, born between a sunset

Jack London was best known for his adventure novels The Call of the Wild, John Barleycorn, *and* The Sea Wolf. *His short story* "An Odyssey of the North," *from which this excerpt is taken, was first published in* The Atlantic Monthly *in 1929; as payment, London received $120 and a one-year subscription to the magazine.*

and a rising, on the dark seas, in my father's oomiak. All of a night the men toiled at the paddles, and the women cast out the waves which threw in upon us, and we fought with the storm. The salt spray froze upon my mother's breast till her breath passed with the passing of the tide. But I,—I raised my voice with the wind and the storm, and lived.

"We dwelt in Akatan"—

"Where?" asked Malemute Kid.

"Akatan, which is in the Aleutians; Akatan, beyond Chignik, beyond Kardalak, beyond Unimak. As I say, we dwelt in Akatan, which lies in the midst of the sea on the edge of the world. We farmed the salt seas for the fish, the seal, and the otter; and our homes shouldered about one another on the rocky strip between the rim of the forest and the yellow beach where our kayaks lay. We were not many, and the world was very small. There were strange lands to the east,—islands like Akatan; so we thought all the world was islands, and did not mind.

"I was different from my people. In the sands of the beach were the crooked timbers and wave-warped planks of a boat such as my people never built; and I remember on the point of the island which overlooked the ocean three ways there stood a pine tree which never grew there, smooth and straight and tall. It is said the two men came to that spot, turn about, through many days, and watched with the passing of the light. These two men came from out of the sea in the boat which lay in pieces on the beach. And they were white like you, and weak as the little children when the seal have gone away and the hunters come home empty. I know of these things from the old men and the old women, who got them from their fathers and mothers before them. These strange white men did not take kindly to our ways at first, but they grew strong, what of the fish and the oil, and fierce. And they built them each his own house, and took the pick of our women, and in time children came. Thus he was born who was to become the father of my father's father.

"As I said, I was different from my people, for I carried the strong, strange blood of this white man who came out of the sea. It is said we had other laws in the days before these men; but they were fierce and quarrel-some, and fought with our men till there were no more left who dared to fight. Then they made themselves chiefs, and took away our old laws and gave us new ones, insomuch that the man was the son of his father, and not his mother, as our way had been. They also ruled that the son, firstborn, should have all things which were his father's before him, and that the brothers and sisters should shift for themselves. And they gave us other laws. They showed us new ways in the catching of fish and the killing of bear which were thick in the woods; and they taught us to lay by bigger stores for the time of famine. And these things were good.

"But when they had become chiefs, and there were no more men to face their anger, they fought, these strange white men, each with the other. And the one whose blood I carry drove his seal spear the length of an arm through the other's body. Their children took up the fight, and their children's children; and there was great hatred between them, and black doings, even to my time, so that in each family but one lived to pass down the blood of them that went before. Of my blood I was alone; of the other man's there was but a girl, Unga, who lived with her mother. Her father and my father did not come back from the fishing one night; but afterward they washed up to the beach on the big tides, and they held very close to each other.

"The people wondered, because of the hatred between the houses, and the old men shook their heads and said the fight would go on when children were born to her and children to me. They told me this as a boy, till I came to believe, and to look upon Unga as a foe, who was to be the mother of children which were to fight with mine. I thought of these things day by day, and when I grew to a stripling I came to ask why this should be so. And they answered, 'We do not know, but that in such way your fathers did.' And I marveled that those which were to come should fight the battles of those that were gone, and in it I could see no right. But the people said it must be, and I was only a stripling.

"And they said I must hurry, that my blood might be the older and grow strong before hers. This was easy, for I was head man, and the people looked up to me because of the deeds and the laws of my fathers, and the wealth which was mine. Any maiden would come to me, but I found none to my liking. And the old men and the mothers of maidens told me to hurry, for even then were the hunters bidding high to the mother of Unga; and should her children grow strong before mine, mine would surely die.

"Nor did I find a maiden till one night coming back from the fishing. The sunlight was lying, so, low and full in the eyes, the wind free, and the kayaks racing with the white seas. Of a sudden the kayak of Unga came driving past me, and she looked upon me, so, with her black hair flying like a cloud of night and the spray wet on her cheek. As I say, the sunlight was full in the eyes, and I was a stripling; but somehow it was all clear, and I knew it to be the call of kind to kind. As she whipped ahead she looked back within the space of two strokes,—looked as only the woman Unga could look,—and again I knew it as the call of kind. The people shouted as we ripped past the lazy oomiaks and left them far behind. But she was quick at the paddle, and my heart was like the belly of a sail, and I did not gain. The wind freshened, the sea whitened, and, leaping like the seals on the windward breech, we roared down the golden pathway of the sun."

Naass was crouched half out of his stool, in the attitude of one driving a paddle, as he ran the race anew. Somewhere across the stove he beheld the tossing kayak and the flying hair of Unga. The voice of the wind was in his ears, and its salt beat fresh upon his nostrils.

"But she made the shore, and ran up the sand, laughing, to the house of her mother. And a great thought came to me that night,—a thought worthy of him that was chief over all the people of Akatan. So, when the moon was up, I went down to the house of her mother, and looked upon the goods of Yash-Noosh, which were piled by the door,—the goods of Yash-Noosh, a strong hunter who had it in mind to be the father of the children of Unga. Other young men had piled their goods there, and taken them away again; and each young man had made a pile greater than the one before.

"And I laughed to the moon and the stars, and went to my own house where my wealth was stored. And many trips I made, till my pile was greater by the fingers of one hand than the pile of Yash-Noosh. There were fish, dried in the sun and smoked; and forty hides of the hair seal, and half as many of the fur, and each hide was tied at the mouth and big-bellied with oil; and ten skins of bear which I killed in the woods when they came out in the spring. And there were beads and blankets and scarlet cloths, such as I got in trade from the people who lived to the east, and who got them in trade from the people who lived still beyond in the east. And I looked upon the pile of Yash-Noosh and laughed; for I was head man in Akatan, and my wealth was greater than the wealth of all my young men, and my fathers had done deeds, and given laws, and put their names for all time in the mouths of the people.

"So, when the morning came, I went down to the beach, casting out of the corner of my eye at the house of the mother of Unga. My offer yet stood untouched. And the women smiled, and said sly things one to the other. I wondered, for never had such a price been offered; and that night I added more to the pile, and put beside it a kayak of well-tanned skins which never yet had swam in the sea. But in the day it was yet there, open to the laughter of all men. The mother of Unga was crafty, and I grew angry at the shame in which I stood before my people. So that night I added till it became a great pile, and I hauled up my oomiak, which was of the value of twenty kayaks. And in the morning there was no pile.

"Then made I preparation for the wedding, and the people that lived even to the east came for the food of the feast and the *potlach* token. Unga was older than I by the age of four suns in the way we reckoned the years. I was only a stripling; but then I was a chief, and the son of a chief, and it did not matter.

"But a ship shoved her sails above the floor of the ocean, and grew larger with the breath of the wind. From her scuppers she ran clear water, and the men were in haste and worked hard at the pumps. On the bow stood a mighty man, watching the depth of the water and giving commands with a voice of thunder. His eyes were of the pale blue of the deep waters, and his head was maned like that of a sea lion. And his hair was yellow, like the straw of a southern harvest or the manila rope-yarns which sailormen plait.

"Of late years we had seen ships from afar, but this was the first to come to the beach of Akatan. The feast was broken, and the women and children fled to the houses, while we men strung our bows and waited with spears in hand. But when the ship's forefoot smelt the beach the strange men took no notice of us, being busy with their own work. With the falling of the tide they careened the schooner and patched a great hole in her bottom. So the women crept back, and the feast went on.

"When the tide rose, the sea wanderers kedged the schooner to deep water, and then came among us. They bore presents and were friendly; so I made room for them, and out of the largeness of my heart gave them tokens such as I gave all the guests; for it was my wedding day, and I was head man in Akatan. And he with the mane of the sea lion was there, so tall and strong that one looked to see the earth shake with the fall of his feet. He looked much and straight at Unga, with his arms folded, so, and stayed till the sun went away and the stars came out. Then he went down to his ship. After that I took Unga by the hand and led her to my own house. And there was singing and great laughter, and the women said sly things, after the manner of women at such times. But we did not care. Then the people left us alone and went home.

"The last noise had not died away, when the chief of the sea wanderers came in by the door. And he had with him black bottles, from which we drank and made merry. You see, I was only a stripling, and had lived all my days on the edge of the world. So my blood became as fire, and my heart as light as the froth that flies from the surf to the cliff. Unga sat silent among the skins in the corner, her eyes wide, for she seemed to fear. And he with the mane of the sea lion looked upon her straight and long. Then his men came in with bundles of goods, and he piled before me wealth such as was not in all Akatan. There were guns, both large and small, and powder and shot and shell, and bright axes and knives of steel, and cunning tools, and strange things the life of which I had never seen. When he showed me by sign that it was all mine, I thought him a great man to be so free; but he showed me also that Unga was to go away with him in his ship. Do you understand?—that Unga was to go away with him in his ship. The blood of my fathers flamed hot on the sudden, and I made to drive him through with my spear. But the spirit of the bottles had stolen the life from my arm, and he took me by the neck, so, and knocked my head against the wall of the house. And I was made weak like a newborn child, and my legs would no more stand under me. Unga screamed, and she laid hold of the things of the house with her hands, till they fell all about us as he dragged her to the door. Then he took her in his great arms, and when she tore at his yellow hair laughed with a sound like that of the big bull seal in the rut.

"I crawled to the beach and called upon my people; but they were afraid. Only Yash-Noosh was a man, and they struck him on the head with an oar, till he lay with his face in the sand and did not move. And they raised the sails to the sound of their songs, and the ship went away on the wind.

"The people said it was good, for there would be no more war of the bloods in Akatan; but I said never a word, waiting till the time of the full moon, when I put fish and oil in my kayak, and went away to the east. I saw many islands and many people, and I, who had lived on the edge, saw that the world was very large. I talked by signs; but they had not seen a schooner nor a man with the mane of a sea lion, and they pointed always to the east. And I slept in queer places, and ate odd things, and met strange faces. Many laughed, for they thought me light of head; but sometimes old men turned my face to the light and blessed me, and the eyes of the young women grew soft as they asked me of the strange ship, and Unga, and the men of the sea.

"And in this manner, through rough seas and great storms, I came to Unalaska. There were two schooners there, but neither was the one I sought. So I passed on to the east, with the world growing ever larger, and in the Island of Unamok there was no word of the ship, nor in Kadiak, nor in Atognak. And so I came one day to a rocky land, where men dug great holes in the mountain. And there was a schooner, but not my schooner, and men loaded upon it the rocks which they dug. This I thought childish, for all the world was made of rocks; but they gave me food and set me to work. When the schooner was deep in the water, the captain gave me money and told me to go; but I asked which way he went, and he pointed south. I made signs that I would go with him; and he laughed at first, but then, being short of men, took me to help work the ship. So I came to talk after their manner, and to heave on ropes, and to reef the stiff sails in sudden squalls, and to take my turn at the wheel. But it was not strange, for the blood of my fathers was the blood of the men of the sea.

"I had thought it an easy task to find him I sought, once I got among his own people; and when we raised the land one day, and passed between a gateway of the sea to a port, I looked for perhaps as many schooners as there were fingers to my hands. But the ships lay against the wharves for miles, packed like so many little fish; and when I went among them to ask for a man with the mane of a sea lion, they laughed, and answered me in the tongues of many peoples. And I found that they hailed from the uttermost part of the earth.

"And I went into the city to look upon the face of every man. But they were like the cod when they run thick on the banks, and I could not count them. And the noise smote upon me till I could not hear, and my head was dizzy with much movement. So I went on and on, through the lands which sang in the warm sunshine; where the harvests lay rich on the plains; and where great cities were fat with men that lived like women, with false words in their mouths and their hearts black with the lust of gold. And all the while my people of Akatan hunted and fished, and were happy in the thought that the world was small.

"But the look in the eyes of Unga coming home from the fishing was with me always, and I knew I would find her when the time was met. She walked down quiet lanes in the dusk of the evening, or led me chases across the thick fields wet with the morning dew, and there was a promise in her eyes such as only the woman Unga could give.

"So I wandered through a thousand cities. Some were gentle and gave me food, and others laughed, and still others cursed; but I kept my tongue between my teeth, and went strange ways and saw strange sights. Sometimes I, who was a chief and the son of a chief, toiled for men,— men rough of speech and hard as iron, who wrung gold from the sweat and sorrow of their fellow men. Yet no word did I get of my quest, till I came back to the sea like a homing seal to the rookeries. But this was at another port, in another country which lay to the north. And there I heard dim tales of the yellow-haired sea wanderer, and I learned that he was a hunter of seals, and that even then he was abroad on the ocean.

"So I shipped on a seal schooner with the lazy Siwashes, and fol-lowed his trackless trail to the north where the hunt was then warm. And we were away weary months, and spoke many of the fleet, and heard much of the wild doings of him I sought; but never once did we raise him above the sea. We went north, even to the Pribyloffs, and killed the seals in herds on the beach, and brought their warm bodies aboard till our scuppers ran grease and blood and no man could stand upon the deck. Then were we chased by a ship of slow steam, which fired upon us with great guns. But we put on sail till the sea was over our decks and washed them clean, and lost ourselves in a fog.

"It is said, at this time, while we fled with fear at our hearts, that the yellow-haired sea wanderer put into the Pribyloffs, right to the factory, and while the part of his men held the servants of the company, the rest loaded ten thousand green skins from the salt-houses. I say it is said, but I believe; for in the voyages I made on the coast with never a meeting, the northern seas rang with his wildness and daring, till the three nations which have lands there sought him with their ships. And I heard of Unga, for the captains sang loud in her praise, and she was always with him. She had learned the ways of his people, they said, and was happy. But I knew better,—knew that her heart harked back to her own people by the yellow beach of Akatan.

"So, after a long time, I went back to the port which is by a gate-way of the sea, and there I learned that he had gone across the girth of the great ocean to hunt for the seal to the east of the warm land which runs south from the Russian Seas. And I, who was become a sailorman, shipped with men of his own race, and went after him in the hunt of the seal. And there were few ships off that new land; but we hung on the flank of the seal pack and harried it north through all the spring of the year. And when the cows were heavy with pup and crossed the Russian line, our men grumbled and were afraid. For there was much fog, and every day men were lost in the boats. They would not work, so the captain turned the ship back toward the way it came. But I knew the yellow-haired sea wanderer was unafraid, and would hang by the pack, even to the Russian Isles, where few men go. So I took a boat, in the black of the night, when the lookout dozed on the fok'slehead, and went alone to the warm, long land. And I journeyed south to meet the men by Yeddo Bay, who are wild and unafraid. And the Yoshiwara girls were small, and bright like steel, and good to look upon; but I could not stop, for I knew that Unga rolled on the tossing floor by the rookeries of the north.

"The men by Yeddo Bay had met from the ends of the earth, and had neither gods nor homes, sailing under the flag of the Japanese. And with them I went to the rich beaches of Copper Island, where our salt-piles became high with skins. And in that silent sea we saw no man till we were ready to come away. Then, one day the fog lifted on the edge of a heavy wind, and there jammed down upon us a schooner, with close in her wake the cloudy funnels of a Russian man-of-war. We fled away on the beam of the wind, with the schooner jamming still closer and plunging ahead three feet to our two. And upon her poop was the man with the mane of the sea lion, pressing the rails under with the canvas and laughing in his strength of life. And Unga was there,—I knew her on the moment,—but he sent her below when the cannons began to talk across the sea. As I say, with three feet to our two, till we saw the rudder lift green at every jump,—and I swinging on to the wheel and cursing, with my back to the Russian shot. For we knew he had it in mind to run before us, that he might get away while we were caught. And they knocked our masts out of us till we dragged into the wind like a wounded gull; but he went on over the edge of the skyline,—he and Unga.

"What could we? The fresh hides spoke for themselves. So they took us to a Russian port, and after that to a lone country, where they set us to work in the mines to dig salt. And some died, and—and some did not die."

Naass swept the blanket from his shoulders, disclosing the gnarled and twisted flesh, marked with the unmistakable striations of the knout. Prince hastily covered him, for it was not nice to look upon.

"We were there a weary time; and sometimes men got away to the south, but they always came back. So, when we who hailed from Yeddo Bay rose in the night and took the guns from the guards, we went to the north. And the land was very large, with plains, soggy with water, and great forests. And the cold came, with much snow on the ground, and no man knew the way. Weary months we journeyed through the endless forest,—I do not remember, now, for there was little food and often we lay down to die. But at last we came to the cold sea, and but three were left to look upon it. One had shipped from Yeddo as captain, and he knew in his head the lay of the great lands, and of the place where men may cross from one to the other on the ice. And he led us,—I do not know, it was so long,—till there were but two. When we came to that place we found five of the strange people which live in that country, and they had dogs and skins, and we were very poor. We fought in the snow till they died, and the captain died, and the dogs and skins were mine. Then I crossed on the ice, which was broken, and once I drifted till a gale from the west put me upon the shore. And after that, Golovin Bay, Pastilik, and the priest. Then south, south, to the warm sunlands where first I wandered

"But the sea was no longer fruitful, and those who went upon it after the seal went to little profit and great risk. The fleets scattered, and the captains and the men had no word of those I sought. So I turned away from the ocean which never rests, and went among the lands, where the trees, the houses, and the mountains sit always in one place and do not move. I journeyed far, and came to learn many things, even to the way of reading and writing from books. It was well I should do this, for it came upon me that Unga must know these things, and that some day, when the time was met—we—you understand, when the time was met.

"So I drifted, like those little fish which raise a sail to the wind, but cannot steer. But my eyes and my ears were open always, and I went among men who traveled much, for I knew they had but to see those I sought, to remember. At last there came a man, fresh from the mountains, with pieces of rock in which the free gold stood to the size of peas, and he had heard, he had met, he knew them. They were rich, he said, and lived in the place where they drew the gold from the ground.

"It was in a wild country, and very far away; but in time I came to the camp, hidden between the mountains, where men worked night and day, out of the sight of the sun. Yet the time was not come. I listened to the talk of the people. He had gone away,—they had gone away,—to England, it was said, in the matter of bringing men with much money together to form companies. I saw the house they had lived in; more like a palace, such as one sees in the old countries. In the nighttime I crept in through a window that I might see in what manner he treated her. I went from room to room, and in such way thought kings and queens must live, it was all so very good. And they all said he treated her like a queen, and many marveled as to what breed of woman she was; for there was other blood in her veins, and she was different from the women of Akatan, and no one knew her for what she was. Ay, she was a queen; but I was a chief, and the son of a chief, and I had paid for her an untold price of skin and boat and bead.

"But why so many words? I was a sailorman, and knew the way of the ships on the seas. I followed to England, and then to other countries. Sometimes I heard of them by word of mouth, sometimes I read of them in the papers; yet never once could I come by them, for they had much money, and traveled fast, while I was a poor man. Then came trouble upon them, and their wealth slipped away, one day, like a curl of smoke. The papers were full of it at the time; but after that nothing was said, and I knew they had gone back where more gold could be got from the ground.

"They had dropped out of the world, being now poor; and so I wandered from camp to camp, even north to the Kootenay Country, where

I picked up the cold scent. They had come and gone, some said this way, and some that, and still others that they had gone to the Country of the Yukon. And I went this way, and I went that, ever journeying from place to place, till it seemed I must grow weary of the world which was so large. But in the Kootenay I traveled a bad trail, and a long trail, with a 'breed' of the Northwest, who saw fit to die when the famine pinched. He had been to the Yukon by an unknown way over the mountains, and when he knew his time was near gave me the map and the secret of a place where he swore by his gods there was much gold.

"After that all the world began to flock into the north. I was a poor man; I sold myself to be a driver of dogs. The rest you know. I met him and her in Dawson. She did not know me, for I was only a stripling, and her life had been large, so she had no time to remember the one who had paid for her an untold price.

"So? You bought me from my term of service. I went back to bring things about in my own way; for I had waited long, and now that I had my hand upon him was in no hurry. As I say, I had it in mind to do my own way; for I read back in my life, through all I had seen and suffered, and remembered the cold and hunger of the endless forest by the Russian Seas. As you know, I led him into the east,—him and Unga,—into the east where many have gone and few returned. I led them to the spot where the bones and the curses of men lie with the gold which they may not have.

"The way was long and the trail unpacked. Our dogs were many and ate much; nor could our sleds carry till the break of spring. We must come back before the river ran free. So here and there we cached grub, that our sleds might be lightened and there be no chance of famine on the back trip. At the McQuestion there were three men, and near them we built a cache, as also did we at the Mayo, where was a hunting-camp of a dozen Pellys which had crossed the divide from the south. After that, as we went on into the east, we saw no men; only the sleeping river, the moveless for-est, and the White Silence of the North. As I say, the way was long and the trail unpacked. Sometimes, in a day's toil, we made no more than eight miles, or ten, and at night we slept like dead men. And never once did they dream that I was Naass, head man of Akatan, the righter of wrongs.

"We now made smaller caches, and in the nighttime it was a small matter to go back on the trail we had broken, and change them in such way that one might deem the wolverines the thieves. Again, there be places where there is a fall to the river, and the water is unruly, and the ice makes above and is eaten away beneath. In such a spot the sled I drove broke through, and the dogs; and to him and Unga it was ill luck, but no more. And there was much grub on that sled, and the dogs the strongest. But he laughed, for he was strong of life, and gave the dogs that were left little grub till we cut them from the harnesses, one by one, and fed them to their mates. We would go home light, he said, traveling and eating from cache to cache, with neither dogs nor sleds; which was true, for our grub was very short, and the last dog died in the traces the night we came to the gold and the bones and the curses of men.

"To reach that place,—and the map spoke true,—in the heart of the great mountains, we cut ice steps against the wall of a divide. One looked for a valley beyond, but there was no valley; the snow spread away, level as the great harvest plains, and here and there about us mighty moun-tains shoved their white heads among the stars. And midway on that strange plain which should have been a valley, the earth and the snow fell away, straight down toward the heart of the world. Had we not been sailor-men our heads would have swung round with the sight; but we stood on the dizzy edge that we might see a way to get down. And on one side, and one side only, the wall had fallen away till it was like the slope of the decks in a topsail breeze. I do not know why this thing should be so, but it was so.

'It is the mouth of hell,' he said; 'let us go down.' And we went down.

"And on the bottom there was a cabin, built by some man, of logs which he had cast down from above. It was a very old cabin; for men had died there alone at different times, and on pieces of birch bark which were there we read their last words and their curses. One had died of scurvy; another's partner had robbed him of his last grub and powder and stolen away; a third had been mauled by a bald-face grizzly; a fourth had hunted for game and starved,—and so it went, and they had been loath to leave the gold, and had died by the side of it in one way or another. And the worthless gold they had gathered yellowed the floor of the cabin like in a dream.

"But his soul was steady, and his head clear, this man I had led thus far. 'We have nothing to eat,' he said, 'and we will only look upon this gold, and see whence it comes and how much there be. Then we will go away quick, before it gets into our eyes and steals away our judgment. And in this way we may return in the end, with more grub, and possess it all.' So we looked upon the great vein, which cut the wall of the pit as a true vein should; and we measured it, and traced it from above and below, and drove the stakes of the claims and blazed the trees in token of our rights. Then, our knees shaking with lack of food, and a sickness in our bellies, and our hearts chugging close to our mouths, we climbed the mighty wall for the last time and turned our faces to the back trip.

"The last stretch we dragged Unga between us, and we fell often, but in the end we made the cache. And lo, there was no grub. It was well done, for he thought it the wolverines, and damned them and his gods in the one breath. But Unga was brave, and smiled, and put her hand in his, till I turned away that I might hold myself. 'We will rest by the fire,' she said, 'till morning, and we will gather strength from our moccasins.' So we cut the tops of our moccasins in strips, and boiled them half of the night, that we might chew them and swallow them. And in the morning we talked of our chance. The next cache was five days' journey; we could not make it. We must find game.

"'We will go forth and hunt,' he said.

"'Yes,' said I, 'we will go forth and hunt.'

"And he ruled that Unga stay by the fire and save her strength. And we went forth, he in quest of the moose, and I to the cache I had changed. But I ate little, so they might not see in me much strength. And in the night he fell many times as he drew into camp. And I too made to suffer great weakness, stumbling over my snowshoes as though each step might be my last. And we gathered strength from our moccasins.

"He was a great man. His soul lifted his body to the last; nor did he cry aloud, save for the sake of Unga. On the second day I followed him, that I might not miss the end. And he lay down to rest often. That night he was near gone; but in the morning he swore weakly and went forth again. He was like a drunken man, and I looked many times for him to give up; but his was the strength of the strong, and his soul the soul of a giant, for he lifted his body through all the weary day. And he shot two ptarmigan, but would not eat them. He needed no fire; they meant life; but his thought was for Unga, and he turned toward camp. He no longer walked, but crawled on hand and knee through the snow. I came to him, and read death in his eyes. Even then it was not too late to eat of the ptarmigan. He cast away his rifle, and carried the birds in his mouth like a dog. I walked by his side, upright. And he looked at me during the moments he rested, and wondered that I was so strong. I could see it, though he no longer spoke; and when his lips moved, they moved without sound. As I say, he was a great man, and my heart spoke for softness; but I read back in my life, and remembered the cold and hunger of the endless forest by the Russian Seas. Besides, Unga was mine, and I had paid for her an untold price of skin and boat and bead.

"And in this manner we came through the white forest, with the silence heavy upon us like a damp sea mist. And the ghosts of the past were in the air and all about us; and I saw the yellow beach of Akatan, and the kayaks racing home from the fishing, and the houses on the rim of the forest. And the men who had made themselves chiefs were there, the law-givers whose blood I bore, and whose blood I had wedded in Unga. Ay, and Yash-Noosh walked with me, the wet sand in his hair, and his war spear, broken as he fell upon it, still in his hand. And I knew the time was met, and saw in the eyes of Unga the promise.

"As I say, we came thus through the forest, till the smell of the camp smoke was in our nostrils. And I bent above him, and tore the ptarmigan from his teeth. He turned on his side and rested, the wonder mounting in his eyes, and the hand which was under slipping slow toward the knife at his hip. But I took it from him, smiling close in his face. Even then he did not understand. So I made to drink from black bottles, and to build high upon the snow a pile of goods, and to live again the things which happened on the night of my marriage. I spoke no word, but he understood. Yet he was unafraid. There was a sneer to his lips, and cold anger, and he gathered new strength with the knowledge. It was not far, but the snow was deep, and he dragged himself very slow. Once, he lay so long, I turned him over and gazed into his eyes. And sometimes he looked forth, and sometimes death. And when I loosed him he struggled on again. In this way we came to the fire. Unga was at his side on the instant. His lips moved, without sound; then he pointed at me, that Unga might understand. And after that he lay in the snow, very still, for a long while. Even now is he there in the snow.

"I said no word till I had cooked the ptarmigan. Then I spoke to her, in her own tongue, which she had not heard in many years. She straightened herself, so, and her eyes were wonder-wide, and she asked who I was, and where I had learned that speech.

"'I am Naass,' I said.

"'You?' she said. 'You?' And she crept close that she might look upon me.

"'Yes,' I answered; 'I am Naass, head man of Akatan, the last of the blood, as you are the last of the blood.'

"And she laughed. By all the things I have seen and the deeds I have done, may I never hear such a laugh again. It put the chill to my soul, sitting there in the White Silence, alone with death and this woman who laughed.

"'Come!' I said, for I thought she wandered. 'Eat of the food and let us be gone. It is a far fetch from here to Akatan.'

"But she shoved her face in his yellow mane, and laughed till it seemed the heavens must fall about our ears. I had thought she would be overjoyed at the sight of me, and eager to go back to the memory of old times; but this seemed a strange form to take.

"'Come!' I cried, taking her strong by the hand. 'The way is long and dark. Let us hurry!'

"'Where?' she asked, sitting up, and ceasing from her strange mirth.

"'To Akatan,' I answered, intent on the light to grow on her face at the thought. But it became like his, with a sneer to the lips, and cold anger.

"'Yes,' she said; 'we will go, hand in hand, to Akatan, you and I. And we will live in the dirty huts, and eat of the fish and oil, and bring forth a spawn,—a spawn to be proud of all the days of our life. We will forget the world and be happy, very happy. It is good, most good. Come! Let us hurry. Let us go back to Akatan.'

"And she ran her hand through his yellow hair, and smiled in a way which was not good. And there was no promise in her eyes.

"I sat silent, and marveled at the strangeness of woman. I went back to the night when he dragged her from me, and she screamed and tore at his hair,—at his hair which now she played with and would not leave. Then I remembered the price and the long years of waiting; and I gripped her close, and dragged her away as he had done. And she held back, even as on that night, and fought like a she-cat for its whelp. And when the fire was between us and the man, I loosed her, and she sat and listened. And I told her of all that lay between, of all that had happened me on strange seas, of all that I had done in strange lands; of my weary quest, and the hungry years, and the promise which had been mine from the first. Ay, I told all, even to what had passed that day between the man and me, and in the days yet young. And as I spoke I saw the promise grow in her eyes, full and large like the break of dawn. And I read pity there, the tenderness of woman, the love, the heart and the soul of Unga. And I was a stripling again, for the look was the look of Unga as she ran up the beach, laughing, to the home of her mother. The stern unrest was gone, and the hunger, and the weary waiting. The time was met. I felt the call of her breast, and it seemed there I must pillow my head and forget. She opened her arms to me, and I came against her. Then, sudden, the hate flamed in her eye, her hand was at my hip. And once, twice, she passed the knife.

"'Dog!' she sneered, as she flung me into the snow. 'Swine!' And then she laughed till the silence cracked, and went back to her dead.

"As I say, once she passed the knife, and twice; but she was weak with hunger, and it was not meant that I should die. Yet was I minded to stay in that place, and to close my eyes in the last long sleep with those whose lives had crossed with mine and led my feet on unknown trails. But there lay a debt upon me which would not let me rest.

"And the way was long, the cold bitter, and there was little grub. The Pellys had found no moose, and had robbed my cache. And so had the three white men; but they lay thin and dead in their cabin as I passed. After that I do not remember, till I came here, and found food and fire,—much fire."

As he finished, he crouched closely, even jealously, over the stove. For a long while the slush-lamp shadows played tragedies upon the wall.

"But Unga!" cried Prince, the vision still strong upon him.

"Unga? She would not eat of the ptarmigan. She lay with her arms about his neck, her face deep in his yellow hair. I drew the fire close, that she might not feel the frost; but she crept to the other side. And I built a fire there; yet it was little good, for she would not eat. And in this manner they still lie up there in the snow."

"And you?" asked Malemute Kid.

"I do not know; but Akatan is small, and I have little wish to go back and live on the edge of the world. Yet is there use in life. I can go to Constantine, and he will put irons upon me, and one day they will tie a piece of rope, so, and I will sleep good. Yet—no; I do not know."

"But, Kid," protested Prince, "this is murder!"

"Hush!" commanded Malemute Kid. "There be things greater than our wisdom, beyond our justice. The right and the wrong of this we cannot say, and it is not for us to judge."

Naass drew yet closer to the fire. There was a great silence, and in each man's eyes many pictures came and went.

EMILY CRAIG ROMIG

A Pioneer Woman in Alaska

THE FOLLOWING DAY we arrived at Nome about noon, but could not go ashore because there were cases of smallpox on some of the boats. However, luck was with us this time, and we were allowed to go ashore at 3:00 P.M. Mr. Craig came out to the boat right away. He had been so worried, because the *Sadie* came in and reported that the *Argo* was lost in the storm and that they had picked up the lighter, so he was glad to see me hale and hearty. He was running a grocery store for Judge Crane on the sand pit. He also had acquired a town lot.

Mrs. Bryant found her husband, but she was not so happy, for the

Emily Craig Romig pioneered through the frozen expanses of southern Alaska in the early 1900s. Her recollections are collected in the autobiography A Pioneer Woman in Alaska *(1945).*

first thing he did was to ask her for twenty-five cents to buy a drink.

Nome was a funny place, with white tents stretched on the beach for miles. We had the nicest store on the spit, and I started in right away to try to learn how to run a store, so as to help as soon as I knew how. Eggs were 50c a dozen; potatoes, 20 pounds for $1.00, while in Dawson eggs were $2.75 a dozen and potatoes 65c a pound.

In order to get to the spit you had to walk over Captain Geiger's bridge—men 10c, women free. As we crossed, two men were quarreling over lot jumping, and each got four or five shots into each other. One died shortly, and the other was soon to die, was the report. The next day they buried one man and talked of lynching the other.

Mr. Carrol called and said he could not get a bed for less than $8.00 a night, and then he would have to wait until the other man got up.

The following day we took a walk up the beach, where the men were rocking gold in their little rockers. There was a rule that a man could place his rocker on any unoccupied part of the beach and no other could come nearer than as far as his spade handle would let him reach, front or back, and to either side of his rocker.

There were many rocking gold. No one needed to be without work or some money, as all he had to do was to get a rocker, a shovel, and a bucket and go out and start working, and be sure to make a good living.

Aug. 18. Mr. Craig having finished our house, we moved in. We had a two-story house and were equipped to run a roadhouse or keep lodgers for the winter.

Later on in the year Mr. Craig, with two partners, went mining up the Kougarok, and located some claims, then came back, as he was no miner. This ground paid about $60,000, but the partners slipped out of the country before we knew they had left.

Mr. Craig went into contracting and building, and did very well for several years. One year he and Miner Bruce secured a boat and went to Siberia trading, but this was not a very good venture and he returned to Nome and followed his trade of building.

In 1903 my brother's daughter, Emily, came to live with us. They pinned or sewed a tag on her back and each conductor signed for her, and the A.C. Co. received her in San Francisco and sent her to Nome in the care of the stewardess of the steamer. She was only eleven years old at the time. We adopted her and she lived with us in Nome until 1909, when we all came back to Seattle, and Mr. Craig went into building and contracting again.

Early in September of 1906 a small ship came to anchor off the town of Nome, Alaska.

Many of the men went to the beach to see who and what it was. A boat was lowered from the side of the ship and proceeded to come ashore. When they reached the beach, two men got out in the water and formed their hands as a chair and carried a third man ashore—this man was Captain Amundsen, and the reason he was carried was that he had on shoes and not high boots as the others.

The ship was the *Gjoa*, the first vessel to make the Northwest Passage from east to west along the Arctic shore of North America.

Soon my husband returned and said the captain and his first officer would have dinner with us—that sounded as though I would be busy for awhile, but I had good help and my daughter knew where all the good silver was and also the fancy linen. My husband brought the two guests and also two other couples from the town. I gave them the best food we had; also hot biscuits, for these were something all men like after being a long while from civilization and home cooking. The dinner passed pleasantly and my ears were wide open. Every Dane or Norwegian, when they are young, has a strain of Viking blood surging in their veins—adventure is music in their ears. Chief Officer Hansen was a Dane, like myself and my husband, and Captain R. Amundsen was from near by—a Norwegian. We spoke the same tongue and all liked the faraway and adventure.

After that, the captain and his first officer came back several times to visit us. The stories of the little boat in uncharted Arctic waters, the moving ice, and the sailing among large ice floes, into leads that might be true and might be false—if false to return before the ice closed in on them and crushed the boat and carried them far into the Arctic—the few Eskimo they visited, and the fresh meat they had to eat, such as bear, seal and caribou, as well as fish and fowl, all had a familiar and interesting sound to us. This was real adventure, and we could visualize the long nights and the starlight, the Northern Lights and the great white solitude.

Captain Amundsen and his party did not tarry long at Nome. However, they had time to have some pictures taken and on September 7, 1906 they came to bid us farewell and each presented us with an autographed picture. Then Captain Amundsen produced a pocket compass and said, "This little instrument I have carried with me every day since I left the shores of Norway. It has been handy to tell me the direction of the movement of ice, the direction of the winds and the course of the flight of birds; also, it has guided me into dusk, gray starlight of the Arctic night when in winter there was no sun, and all day was night. It helped us to go out for wood, game and for the necessary walks and recreation. It helped us to come back to the ship, and in fact was a true and tried friend. I will not need it any longer and I wish you would accept this in memory of our visit with you and with thanks for your hospitality."

I took it, and said, "It will always remind me of you and your voyage and that it has played a small part in this historic adventure."

More than thirty years later my husband and I were strolling down the beach below the Cliff House at San Francisco. There in a little cove, near some trees, was a boat. The boat rested above ground on a cradle, the sails were all gone and just the bare rigging remained, but her bow pointed out to see, as much to say: "I am ready for another voyage."

As we drew near I noticed on her bow, *Gjoa*. Right then it seemed I had met a long lost friend from over the seas, an old country friend. When last I saw her, she was riding proudly off the beach of Nome, Alaska, and now, her skipper long since passed away and the crew scattered, there she stood as a monument to that eventful voyage, far from her native shores. I, like the boat, also seemed so far from my native shore. My first husband had passed; the crossing of the Atlantic; and after that, the long trip from Chicago to Nome overland—two years and ten months of rugged travel in the Arctic—where would I find my resting place. I do not know how long I stood in this state of reverie. Few knew and no one seemed to care for the boat and its heroic history. I thought—are people like boats?

Then I came to myself and looked up. Near me was my husband, his hat in his hand, the sea breeze playing with his white hair, he seemed to be thinking, too. I did not speak, but looked at him, and thought—"You, too, have ridden the Boundless Main in many rough places and felt the sting of cold winds and frosty spray; you, also, have traveled many dreary Arctic trails and camped in cold and lonesome places."

INTERVIEWS WITH ALASKANS

MONTY RICHARDSON
Earthquake!, Seward, b. 1918

ALASKANS REACTED TO *the earthquake devastation of Good Friday
1964 with characteristic resourcefulness and gumption. The epicenter of this
megatrembler was beneath Miners Lake in northern Prince William Sound.
Eleven people died at Seward, a railhead port of twenty-three hundred people, many taverns, and innumerable fishing stories. Today Monty
Richardson is a familiar figure on the rebuilt waterfront, where he hires out
his 1978 Chris Craft, the Irish Lord, to sports fishermen. Monty retired in
1976 from a teaching career that began in a Colorado one-room schoolhouse. But his greatest challenge came not in the classroom or at the tiller but
on the streets of Seward.*

These self-portraits are excerpted from Alaskans: Life on the Last Frontier.
*Edited by Ron Strickland, the book is a collection of interviews with seventy
modern-day Alaskans, from a Bonehead whale hunter to an Eskimo judge.*

I'D GONE THROUGH drought and dust storm in Oklahoma back in the drought-ridden thirties, and I had had about all I wanted of that. And I felt the lure of the last frontier, the uncrowded vistas, and the hunting, fishing, so I talked the wife into it. I loaded her and two kids in the station wagon and brought all of our earthly belongings over the Alcan. It was quite rough, you bet! It was all gravel. We busted a windshield and busted the trailer way out in the wilderness of the Yukon. We had a lot of adversities here and there but we've never regretted a minute of it.

In my early days in Seward, there was a lot of elbow-bending. There still is. Seward is a hard-drinking town. In winter it's cold and dark and not many diversions. Yeah, this is still pretty much of a free and open town. A lot of dissipation goes on. Always has.

My wife is a good old solid part-Cherokee Indian. I guess you could call us Okies. Yeah, although in 1956 we had never been to California. That's what the true making of an Okie was in the Dust Bowl, having been to California. We went to Alaska instead of California, and by 1964 we were both working in the schools here and we called Seward home.

On Good Friday I was up at the house, 519 Third Avenue, in the middle of Seward at five thirty-seven in the afternoon. I'd been ill with the flu. Fortunately there was no school that day because it was Good Friday. I had finally gotten up out of bed to get to the barber shop before six o'clock to get my hair cut. I walked outside and a friend, a local policeman, stopped by to chat a few minutes. When the earthquake hit—we had had earthquakes right along—we both remarked casually about here was another one. But then it increased in intensity, and when I saw his tires bouncing off the ground in that undulating, rolling motion, why I knew something serious was happening.

It was such a long, long four minutes. Nine point two on today's Richter scale! North America's most powerful earthquake ever recorded.

About a minute and a half into the earthquake, why Standard Oil's big gasoline storage tanks blew sky-high. Flames and smoke went hundreds of feet into the air. My friend roared out of my driveway and lurched down the street in his police car to the waterfront.

I remember looking up and seeing the top of Mount Marathon just trembling and trembling like it was going to tumble right down on us. And as the shaking went on and on and on, the thirty-five-foot-high chimney on the grade school across the street from us swayed back and forth and back and forth until in slow motion it came, whumpf, roaring down. Our own chimney bricks almost hit me in the head. Finally the wife and kids stumbled outside and we huddled and huddled while everything fell around us.

Fires raced down Seventh Avenue and caught fire to thirty-one loaded fuel tank cars that had overturned. And they all went off like the most giant firecrackers you can imagine. The wife and I decided we'd better get out of town before we got roasted. I did have presence of mind enough to shut our electricity off and grab some clothing. By the time we got out of town and drove to the head of the bay, the pavement was wet from a high tide, but we figured we were safe. Half an hour after the earthquake, about seventy-five or a hundred other people were milling around there watching the tanks explode and buildings catch fire.

Nobody was thinking straight, of course, but the tide was way, way out. I had never seen so many mud flats! That should have told us that if it went out, it was darned sure going to come back in. And then I saw a big, white frothy mass out in the bay. I thought, "Well, what's all that snow doing out there?" We were looking up the bay toward Fox Islands about twelve miles out at what looked like a bunch of snow on the bay. I couldn't figure out . . . I had never seen anything like that, though I had been on the bay many times. Then soon, even with the crackling of the fires and people chattering excitedly, I began to hear like a freight train in the distance. And then it got louder and louder. Then we could see skip, skip, skip just like a snow avalanche coming down a mountainside. Well, it began to dawn on people what it was! A *tidal wave*. And it was really barreling in. We finally began to yell, "tidal wave," and started running away from the beach to our cars. Several didn't make it. They got killed right there on the spot. One old couple, a man and his wife, I can still see 'em, just frantic. They couldn't get their car started. Flooded it or something. And they were killed.

We were racing as fast as we could up a little old, dim dirt road, right straight away from the bay, or we wouldn't be here to tell the story. All sorts of timber and boats and debris came crashing down around us and we just barely got away.

We drove about a mile farther to a place called The Three Bridges, where the Resurrection River divides into three parts. And that was as far as we could go because the earth had sunk six foot and there were the bridges hanging up in the air.

We and the other people turned around and came back, but not too far back because the fires and tidal waves had everybody panic-stricken. My wife remembered that she had the key to the little four-room school where she taught a mile and a half out of town. So we decided to go up there. No way could we get back into town because the tidal wave had thrown monstrous amounts of debris across the road. So we opened up the schoolhouse, not knowing what we would get in the way of wounded people or even dead people. Sure enough, people came straggling in there. Some with bruises and scratches but nobody badly hurt. About a hundred fifty adults and children spent a harrowing night in that schoolhouse.

All the facilities were overburdened almost immediately, so we decided to go up to an old Quonset hut where the government had stored some civil defense supplies years back and see what we could get to help take care of all the people. We took flashlights and jumped over some big earthquake fissures and knocked the door in. Big, old wooden crates were stacked to the ceiling. They had codes on 'em but we didn't know what the codes were, so we heaved and struggled and got a couple into my van and got them back to the schoolhouse, hoping that we had some stuff for food or shelter or warmth. But when we pried open the first crate, it was full of bedpans.

The four toilets were plugged almost immediately, so along about midnight we eased back down to the bay to get some water to flush those toilets out. We started walking and walking out across the mud and sand to fill our garbage cans. We should have known. . . . Earlier in the evening should have told us that if we had to go that far out in the mud with no real water there, then, by golly, the bay, it had run out again, tilted, and was sure going to come back in. But we were a little bit wary by that time. When we heard that roar coming, why we threw our garbage cans down and took to our heels and got out of there. We came within an inch of getting caught in another tidal wave that came roaring in like a freight train. We got out of there with our lives just before it came crashing in.

Twice in about six hours we had almost got caught in tidal waves. Again the monstrous force threw all sorts of debris up in the timber. It threw a freight car clear over across the bluff, a mile away from the beach.

We stayed in the school all night. Nobody slept because the after-shocks came on with terrifying frequency. Every ten or fifteen minutes a booming aftershock hit. We heard about five tidal waves come crashing in. Some people became hysterical, afraid the waves would come up there and get us. The beach was a mile away but we didn't know what to expect and women and children screamed each time another one roared in.

During the night a few people reached us from town over Mount Marathon, winding their way through the timber and the snow. They told us wild stories about how much of the town had burned.

At daylight we were able to ease our way back to town through an eight- or ten-foot-wide strip bulldozed through the debris. We found that the fires had laid a massive layer of soot on the streets and snow. Our foundation was cracked, the chimney had tumbled down. The back porch had pulled away from the main house. It was just a royal mess inside. Broken glass and dishes and pottery, fallen shelves, stuff all smashed up.

Yet we were lucky to be in the center of Seward. Houses down along the waterfront were totally destroyed by the tidal waves and fires. For a small community of seventeen or eighteen hundred people, some eighty-five to ninety homes were completely demolished.

Yet we never thought of leaving, even though we didn't know if we still had teaching jobs or not. I had a wife and three small children to support, and fortunately the schools were only closed ten or twelve days. The Civil Defense and military jumped right in and began repairing the high school to use it to house and feed people. They didn't want anybody lighting fires here in town. There was no water. Most of the chimneys and flues and heating systems had been shattered and they didn't want anybody to light fires. So they went up and down the streets with bullhorns encouraging everybody to take their meals at the army field kitchen at the high school. Some people whose homes had been destroyed were bedded down there on cots for a goodly number of days and nights.

After about two weeks they were able to patch up all three schools enough to where we could get through the rest of the year. So we teachers were only out about fourteen days. The authorities wanted to do something with the great amounts of kids that were wandering around getting in the way of cleaning up the debris and getting the facilities of the town working again.

The people of Seward showed real intestinal fortitude. I'd say the majority of them were gutsy people that pitched in and cooperated and helped solve the problems. However, Alaskans come in all stripes. Unfortunately there were a few, as there would be in any community, that instead of helping solve the problems, they added to the problems.

For days and days we were isolated because there is only one road out of here and it was shattered. Of course, the only planes that were flying in here on a damaged airfield were military and Civil Defense. But some people, by golly, with all those aftershocks still coming on and the town just devastated, they took off and they left and they never came back. But the majority of them, even though everything was gone and they had not much more than the clothes on their back, they all pitched in and started building their lives again.

The wife and I wanted to stay because by that time we had been in Alaska seven years. Alaska was good to us. We liked it. We were getting our roots down. When we sized the situation up, we knew that it was going to be a long, tough struggle, but we felt we were equal to it. In many respects the town became better after the earthquake. Gutsy people rebuilt everything bigger and better and more prosperous than it had been before. The federal government gave us a new small boat harbor, the commercial harbor, and other facilities. And the Red Cross, Salvation Army, Civil Defense, and other agencies pitched in and by midsummer we were beginning to struggle to our feet.

Today we earthquake survivors all have our own phantoms to chase. Many of us are fatalistic: "If it's going to happen, it will." If Seward people were worried about earthquakes, they'd go someplace else. In 1964 the wife and I, we didn't really have anything to go back to Outside. We had cut all ties when we left there in '56. Things had not been too good for us Outside and Alaska had become our home and our future.

~

SADIE BROWER NEAKOK

Iñupiaq Judge, Barrow, b. 1916

MISPERCEPTIONS BETWEEN NATIVE *and Anglo individuals have long been an undercurrent of northern life, often with tragic results. Sadie Brower Neakok is an inspiring teacher, welfare worker, and judge who has not only bridged the gap between the Eskimo and white cultures but also made it easier for others to move between these two poles of Alaskan life.*

Charles Brower was the first white settler in Barrow, America's northernmost town. He operated a whaling station there in the late nineteenth century and a fur-trading post thereafter. He married an Eskimo woman named Asianggataq and had ten children, including Sadie Bower. Educated Outside, Sadie returned to Barrow, married an Iñupiaq whaler named Nate Neakok, and raised thirteen children of her own plus many foster children. Sadie was appointed to be a bush magistrate in 1960, and her work eventually established the precedent of using Native languages in court when the defendant did not know English. The following reflections are taken from Margaret B. Blackman's Sadie Brower Neakok: An Iñupiaq Woman.

THERE WERE BLUNDERS, too, in my work, where I got so scared, going forward on my own without any orders. Like we were instructed to never use our native language in court, but here was this man who couldn't speak a word of English. The state trooper brought this charge before me, and I arraigned the man. What had happened was that he was charged with petit larceny, taking something away from the base area that was surplus, that to his mind was good stuff that he was going to put to use with his family who needed it. But he didn't tell the superiors that he was going to take some of the stock, and when the state trooper apprehended him, he knew he had made a mistake, and he refunded everything that he had taken.

But here this case came up, and the trooper never told me any-thing about him refunding the stock, and he pled guilty. I was speaking my native tongue all the time. I advised him of his rights, and he said he didn't want to use his rights, he wanted to waive them and admit to the charge that was before him. We did it in such a manner it was on record—tape—and I had to interpret the whole thing so the court system would know what the case was about. But I didn't know that base up there was federal property, and the trooper made a state charge instead of a federal charge out of it. So four days later the federal authorities arrest this man and take him to Anchorage before a federal court. I got this phone call over at the Wien Airlines terminal from the chief justice of the Alaska Court System about that case.

I was asked to come to Anchorage and demonstrate how I arraigned this man. "Did I, in fact, have so-and-so in my court on a charge?" "Yes. The state trooper brought the charge, and I heard it, and this case was disposed of." "Well, we want you to come down and demonstrate before the federal courts how you did it." I had to go down there. And I had never been in a big courthouse, let alone in a robe. And they railroaded me into this big courthouse and put a robe on me, and as the prisoner was brought in, we all had to stand for the gavel. This we did in my court when I came in, but not that formally. My heart was in my throat. I explained that I did it all in my native tongue because there was no alternative. There was no way that I could make this man understand what his rights were until I used his own native language.

So they bring in the prisoner, and who should it be but the same man I had arraigned who didn't know one word of English. As they brought him in he was looking down, and he looked up and he recognized me and you should have seen the beam on his face: "Hi, Sadie!" Right there in the courthouse. No formality of any kind, not knowing why he was being brought there, but recognizing me. He didn't even know I was there, but when he looked up and recognized me, the smile on his face, and then for him to say, "Hi, Sadie!"

And then I demonstrated. Well, after I demonstrated to them, I told him in Eskimo, "We have to go all through the same thing we went through in Barrow." And he did beautifully. He pled guilty. And then I asked the state trooper what was the charge there, was this true? Because when someone gives himself up to me on a plea of guilty of an admission of guilt or *nolo contendere*, then you ask the defendant if he has anything to say where we might show cause for leniency. He came up with the statement that he did let the trooper know that he [had] returned all the items he was charged with, and [that] they were back at the base. And then I asked the trooper, "Is this true?" He said, "Yes, it is true." "Well, why didn't you mention it?" And then they knew what kind of person I was. I wanted the full information on any case that came up before me. I told them I was stumped: I couldn't read his rights in English; he couldn't make heads nor tails out of it; and he didn't know anything about the law, nor did he know that he stole. He was just taking something that was going to be thrown away—he just took advantage of it—and so, all those things, they [had] never [come] out.

The court system had planted some people in the back, listeners who were from my town, to record and to translate back in English what I had said in court about the man's rights. When it was all over, I was told, "The chief justice would like to see you in his chambers." My heart is still in my throat, and I thought, "This is where I get thrown out." I was so scared. But when I got to his door, there he was in a white shirt just relaxing, smoking his pipe in his chamber. And he said, "Hi, Sadie." The voice that he greeted me with had no hurt in it whatsoever, and he said, "That was the most wonderful demonstration you performed. From now on, it will be a rule of the court to use the language of the people." So from there on [c. 1964], they started using the native language.

Having been born and grown up here, there was a time when there wasn't drinking. It started coming up after the base was settled. Our menfolks and our young people started consuming alcohol, and I could see where the fights were coming from—assault and battery, assault with dangerous weapon, or whatever. The laws say that you cannot use alcohol as an excuse and bring it into court—"Because I was drunk, I don't remember doing it." Well, you can't use leniency, because he was drunk and did this. In evaluating cases, most of the time, if that type of complaint came in and it was signed by some member of [the] family caught in the same situation [also drunk], automatically when they sobered up, they were no longer fighting, they were friends again. If they had broken anything, if they had wrecked something, I would take the criminal charge away, and let them pay restitution, and just let them go—with warnings that they could go to jail for a certain amount of months or days the next time. And it worked. So, much of my feeling went into my work, and I talked to my people. And knowing them was even harder, because I couldn't believe some of the charges against my own people, when the law says drunkenness is no excuse to do an act. That was even harder for my people to believe, when they sobered up, that they did something like that. Shameful.

My main concern in that job was to make my people learn about the law, and to learn about what rights they had. Some would be mad at me, because they were held in jail and didn't know what their rights were. At arraignments they would ask, "What is that?" And it used to take me fifteen or twenty minutes longer to try and explain and make my people understand what their rights were—rights to a lawyer, rights to remain silent, and oh, they had many rights that I had to read them. And when that initial period was over, then it was much easier for me to hold court. And when the city adopted all the misdemeanor laws as city ordinances, on Monday mornings my courthouse was like a schoolhouse. I had so many the police had picked up over the weekend, when liquor first came into Barrow in the early sixties, and I had to find out a system to take care of each and every one of those as fast as I could. So I used to let them line up in front of me, and I divided them into who could understand English and who could not understand English. I was asked to use my native tongue to make them understand what their rights were. So, I could read their rights to the ones who were able to speak English and understand it, and have them line up. And then the ones who were not able to understand fully what the English language was all about, then I would do it in my native tongue. And then their charges are right in front of me; so like a school roll call, I would call each name and ask them, one by one. And when a person admitted to the charge before me, there were set fines. If it was an ordinance-violation [that] the city had given me on a first offender, it was a suspended sentence. If the same offense was committed for a second time that month, then a ten dollar fine. The third one, the fine tripled, until you had five or six charges against you. Then it became a state matter, instead of a city ordinance.

I was in the habit of searching for solutions to better our situations, because by Monday I would have thirty or forty cases in the morning—the same alcohol-related charges. The police that we had there would just throw them in jail. Or, if they were transporting liquor while under the influence, that was another charge—one of the ordinances, too. You could just walk out your door here with a can of beer and get arrested. Your property didn't mean that you were in your own private property—didn't mean a thing to the police, because we didn't own our property then. We were squatters on the land until BIA decided they would give us the lots and area where our houses were, and they were sectioned off. But before that it was such that you were a violator under the city ordinances, and I was collecting all these fines and making some six or seven thousand dollars a month at the time for the city through their ordinances, because the fines stayed in the community. In those days the menfolks and most everyone in this community were earning big wages, and those fines didn't mean a thing. It wasn't a punishment to them. They would go back, walk out of the courthouse and do the same thing, and they would be right back in my courthouse. They just handed the fine over, and the city was getting richer fast from those ordinance violations.

So, when that didn't seem like a punishment to the people, then I went to the council and asked if there were some way we could put these people on a work release program, clean up program, or help out somebody in need with building their home, or whatever. And oh, you should have seen the effects of that one. People who came from well-respected families, said, "Oh, I'm not going to be seen out there doing silly work— clean up or. . . ." "Either that, or you sit in jail." It was a choice. And that jail we had wasn't a very pleasant place to be. The solution wasn't very popular, and people hated me for that, because people who classed themselves well-to-do did not like to be seen out there in the street, cleaning up because they had been picked up. That was the most effective sentencing in those times, to put somebody on a work-release program. People didn't like it, and they started thinking about themselves.

In the matter of sentencing, I waited until I looked into the family situation. Sometimes this is [unorthodox], but it was my practice. I knew the people, but I had to get more information—why this was happening, if it was a repeated offense. If I had to sentence a person on their plea of guilty, or if they were found guilty, I had to look into the background of the family, or ask question of the defendant after the case was all formed, that might allow me to show leniency or give me an idea what type of sentencing would be proper. Then I would have to explain why I am giving it. It helped to look into the family matters at times.

In areas like Fairbanks and Anchorage my system would never work, because I wouldn't know the people. But I made it a point, if I didn't know the person standing before me, to ask them questions—where he is from, and how long he has been here, and how long he expects to stay, and what type of work he is doing—those types of questions. I wanted to know the whole story so I could evaluate the case properly before me and get to the core of it, what caused it. And after a plea of guilty or a no-contest plea, then I could ask the person to give me his views, what he felt, talk to me freely so it wouldn't happen again. They did talk freely; they never kept back. And later on, some of the whites who were looking down on me got to know me better. They didn't shun me anymore. That was quite hard to come to, and they found me a different person. Sometimes they would knock on my door and come in and apologize for their attitude.

∿

KELLEY WEAVERLING
Oil Spill Wildlife Rescue, Cordova, b. 1946

ONE OF THE *most televised aspects of the* Exxon Valdez *oil spill on March 24, 1989, was the wildlife rescue effort. About two hundred fifty people, fifty vessels, and numerous aircraft were mobilized to bring oiled birds and animals out of the wilds for emergency care. The man in charge of this flotilla was Kelley Weaverling, a Californian who has lived beside Prince William Sound since 1976. Because of his years guiding kayak trips through the area, Kelley was a natural choice for admiral of this ragtag fleet. Eventually the wildlife crisis propelled Kelley into politics. Although he had considered himself an environmentalist before the oil spill, he felt compelled by the catastrophe to leave the sidelines and jump into the fray. In 1991 he was elected mayor of Cordova.*

THEY CALLED ME at our bookstore—coffee shop in Cordova on the twenty-eighth of March. We collected our first oiled bird on the thirtieth during our initial reconnaissance trip. Nobody knows for sure, but we guess that as many as three hundred thousands birds were lost during the oil spill.

Lots and lots of my special places were ruined. Like the place where I met my wife, Susan Ogle, in 1977. There's a lot of trade and barter in Alaska and that's how we met. We were both artists, making our living in Anchorage during the wintertime in graphic arts. At an office party I traded her one of my guided kayak trips for some artwork for my new brochure. But that early spring shakedown trip, the first one of the season, when I was trying to remember what it is like to guide people, was not particularly conducive to romance. It was very rainy and very cold, early in the spring with snow still on the beach. And there were a lot of people. Actually Susan and I were thrown together in one tent because we had to deal with a couple of hypothermic bear hunters who came up to where we were camped real wet and hypothermic. So the bear hunters got my tent and I had to share Susan's tent. That's when and how we fell in love!

So the oil spill was very personal, you bet! You hear about break-ins and vandalism and you think it's bad. But when it happens to your house . . . I had been on almost every beach that was hit by the spill.

As far as I can tell, Exxon's total plan for wildlife was to make two phone calls. One to SeaWorld and one to the international birds rescue center. The International Bird Rescue and Research Center out of Berkeley has been doing this sort of activity for many years. They're kind of like the Red Adair of the bird world. When there's a spill, they're called out, and they're real good at what they do. It was just that the logistics, collection and delivery, in this remote and harsh environment were beyond their experiences. That's why they called me.

After I had sketched out a plan over the telephone, I went next-door to Cordova District Fishermen United (CDFU) and got three fishing vessels and their skippers and some crew members. I made some phone calls to some friends of mine in Anchorage who were real familiar with Prince William Sound and had them meet me the next morning at seven in Valdez. I motored all night long to get there on time.

In Valdez we made contact with the bird rescue people. We collected one more vessel and went out into the spill to figure out the best way to collect and deliver these birds.

We found out how big an area one small strike force could deal with, and then I went back to Cordova and drew up a plan to cover the impacted area. I estimate the number of boats and personnel that would be required and I had it okayed by the bird rescue center. And then I began dispatching vessels.

At first the oil spill transcended all the existing problems, and everything else was out the window. It was beautiful to see the community coalesce instantly in the face of a large disaster like this. But it was only later, when Exxon came and VECO, that the community began to split again when some people began to benefit more than others.

My own motivation was that I had been interested in the out-of-doors all of my life. As a young boy, I had related to nature largely as a physical challenge, looking for difficult climbing routes. But just through being in that environment, my awareness increased to other aspects, to the interrelatedness of the environment out there.

I was born and raised in California. I came to Alaska largely to get away from the world at large. To find a place to hide out and to live in a community which was real and not a tourist town. Just before I came here, I had spent the previous four years wandering around Europe, climbing in the summertime around Zermatt and Chamonix and skiing in the wintertime. Then my wife and I operated a summer-long kayak guide service in Prince William Sound from 1976 until 1980. In 1980 we decided that we didn't care to guide kayak trips anymore because we just liked going out kayaking by ourselves.

So we arranged our lives in such a way that in April of each year we packed all our belongings in cardboard boxes, bought four months' worth of food, cached the food, and stayed out from the first of May until the end of August. From 1981 until 1987.

Three or four months continuous out in the sound. We became very familiar with the area and documented all our travels. All the beaches and wildlife.

Many of the orcas out there I recognize as individuals. I have known some of them longer than I have known a lot of my friends here in Alaska.

That's why the oil spill affected me so much. But out on the rescue everybody cried two or three times a day. You couldn't help it. You just got overcome. It was horrible beyond description. But we had to keep on. If we didn't do it, who would?

MARGARET MURIE

Geese

"WILL YOU LOVE me in December as you do in May?"

     Jess was standing on the decked-over bow of the scow, poling and singing. He had a very nice high tenor voice. I love to sing too. We both knew hundreds of songs, and I really believe this saved our sanity, our friendship, and the success of the expedition. Down on the floor of the scow, just behind Jess, the baby and I spent our days now in a four-by-four space under the light muslin-and-netting tent a field naturalist friend in Washington had insisted we take along. Life from June 29 on would have been fairly intolerable without it. Here in this space were the baby's

Margaret Murie was the first woman graduate of the University of Alaska in Fairbanks. With her husband, biologist Olaus Murie, she dedicates herself to conservation of the wild. She is the author of Two in the Far North *(1957), from which "Geese" is taken.*

box, beside it Olaus's collector's trunk, and, piled on the trunk, all the baby paraphernalia and other small articles needed during the day. My stool was set in front of the chest, beside the box. And that was all; this was our world. By leaning forward and putting my eyes close to the net-ting, I could catch glimpses of the outside world. It remained unvaried for five weeks: Jess's booted legs, the tip of the red-painted bow, a green blur of grass and willows on the shore, maybe a bit of sky. Sometimes I caught a view of Olaus, trudging along on shore, the line over his shoulder. He was "pulling her by the whiskers," as the trappers say; Jess, experienced with the pike pole, leaned his weight on every stroke in a steady rhythm, all day long.

So we slid along, and sang song after song, and estimated our progress, trying to pick out landmarks from the Geological Survey maps. But the Old Crow throughout its middle course has no landmarks; just high banks, brown stream, green shore.

Variation came when Olaus would signal frantically from shore. The song would stop in mid phrase. Then we would quickly haul up the canoe, and both men would get in and push off, after a flock of flightless young geese which by now would have taken fright and would be beating furiously through the water. By this time I would be out on the bow, pole in hand. "If we're gone too long, try to get to shore where you can hook a wil-low, and wait for us"—the parting shot as canoe, men, and geese disap-peared around a bend upstream.

It was fortunate that the Old Crow *was* a sluggish stream. The scow drifted now toward one shore, now toward the other. I wound the bandanas tighter over my shirt cuffs to keep mosquitoes from crawling in, tied the strings of the head net tighter about my chest, leaned on the pole, and waited. If the slow current took us close to shore, I reached out and caught a branch with the hook. Then it was just sit there on the bow and hold it. If it were near Martin's mealtime and he began to call and fret, I could only pray that the bird banders would appear again sometime.

In ten minutes—or an hour—they would come, bringing a new story. "Hey, you should have seen your husband up there in the mud, trying to catch up with an old goose before he got over the bank." Or: "Jess should have been a football player; he made a peach of a flying tackle after two young ones. Well, that's six for us already today."

Sometimes the canoe would come in fast, sliding up to the scow, and Olaus would reach over and dump a gunny sack at my feet. "Don't worry; they won't hurt one another. We're going after another bunch up here."

The banders' advantage was that in these weeks the adult geese had shed their wing feathers and the young had not yet grown theirs, so that all were flightless.

One hot day the sack contained six full-grown but flightless geese. For forty interminable minutes I drifted, and poled, and watched the river in vain for the canoe, while those poor creatures never stopped squawking and wriggling. It was a big surprise for me when, after finally being banded, they all went down the stream again honking furiously, and unhurt.

Lunch was more ordeal than pleasure during these weeks. The men would try to build a fire for tea, but the willow, so much of it green, was poor fuel. Some days we merely went ashore with the tin grub box and ate a bowl of stewed fruit or tomatoes with pilot biscuits or cold sourdough pancakes and a bit of cheese. Bowl in hand, you loosened the string of the head net, poked the spoonful of food into your mouth, and quickly let the net down again. It was the same with all the bites. Even so, there'd be a few bugs to squash inside the net when lunch was over! This was merely taking in fuel for energy; it was no social hour.

Down in the tiny haven on the scow I heated mush or tomatoes or a bit of gravy on the Sterno outfit for Martin. He never came out of there until we camped at night. That is why we had to let him crawl about the tent as long as he liked in the evenings, and why Olaus romped and played with him every night. It was his only exercise during those five weeks.

Olaus has a biologist's scorn of allowing anything biological to disturb him. All creatures are a legitimate part of the great pattern he believes in and lives by. He ignored the mosquitoes with a saintly manner that made me furious at times. But one day he paid!

He and Jess had been chasing a long white-fronted goose for a long time. As it was the first white-fronted goose of the season, it was worth a lot of time and effort. Olaus finally went ashore under a steep mud bank and waited for Jess to drive the goose to him with the canoe. From across the river, where I had hooked a willow, I watched the play. The goose swam upstream, Jess after it. Just as he came close enough to hope to turn its course, the goose dived. Jess waited and watched. As soon as the goose came up he paddled hard, trying to get ahead of it and force it to swim toward Olaus. The goose dived.

This went on for a half an hour. Every line of Jess's figure as he swung the paddle expressed determination; even under his head net I could see how his long jaw was set. The goose seemed fresh as a daisy. It rose each time with a quick sidewise glance at the canoe and a Bronx-cheer kind of honk.

Once she came up very near the scow. Jess came tearing past, talking to the goose. "God damn you, I'll get you if we have to go clear to the canyon together!"

Away they went around the bend; Olaus waved to me from across the stream, the kind of wave that said: "This is a funny life we're in, isn't it!"

Then the goose came swimming back again, paddling furiously, honking a little anxiously; right behind her Jess, also paddling furiously. And this time she decided shore was the place.

Olaus had lifted his net to watch the performance, and had also taken off his gloves—something Jess or I would never have done. Now he had to freeze into position, for the goose had begun to wade ashore at the spot where he was crouching. It padded determinedly up the bank. Suddenly it became aware of the figure there and hesitated. "Onk?" it questioned, and waited, watching Olaus. Then it put one web foot forward in the mud. "Onk?" again. Olaus didn't dare move an eyelid. Mosquitoes were setting in black clouds on his face and hands.

Out in the stream sat Jess, at ease in the canoe. Now it was his turn; he could make all the noise he wanted; he had forgotten his awful anger at that goose. "Heh, heh, heh," he said in his high-pitched voice. "How you like the mosquitoes, eh? Nice comfortable position you're in, isn't it?"

Olaus kept silent; he was as determined to get this bird as Jess was. The bird took another very tentative step, looked at Olaus, and asked him again: "Onk?" No answer. From out on the river: "Boy, don't you wish you'd kept your net on! How long d'you think this will take? Watch her now!"

The goose took three steps; it was feeling the nearness of the over-hung bank and safety above it. Like a fox drawing his legs up imperceptibly for a pounce, Olaus moved his feet, so carefully. "Onk?" Spring! Pounce! He had it round the body by both hands; they were sliding down the slippery mud together, and Jess was whooping: "Hang on, don't let her slip—I'm coming! How do your mosquito bites feel? Boy, don't anybody ever say anything to me about foolish as a goose; they're about the smartest damn critters you can find!"

They were slow, strenuous hours, chasing geese like this. Yet practically every goose we saw was caught and banded. Either the Old Crow had been much overrated as a nesting ground or something strange had happened in 1926, for we never found the "hundreds of thousands" someone had described to the powers in Washington. The days were hot and muggy, and we felt almost a claustrophobia down there between those steep banks and thawing Pleistocene mud, in a steaming, whining breathless world where insects were in full command. We human creatures were saved from insanity and death only by a few yards of cheese cloth and netting and leather. Sometimes the shield felt pretty thin. We longed for a breeze with passionate longing and welcomed a hard shower, because it downed the hordes for a while; and at least it substituted the sound of water for that other perpetual sound.

"NOTICE HOW MUCH lower the banks are today? I think we're getting into different country." Olaus, always hopeful, always optimistic, was poling today.

Jess was on the line, over on the lower shore. His answer was prompt: "Can't be different country any too damn soon for me."

Five o'clock—the banks still lower, a clear sky. "Hey, Mardy, feel the breeze?"

I scrambled out from my "hole." What a feeling! Moving air! I looked up; the solid cloud of spiraling insects were gone; the wind had dispersed their formation, broken their absolute control of the land. "Can't I go ashore and walk a little? Martin's asleep."

I fell into step behind Jess, shoulder under the line. "Sure a lot more current here," he said. "Maybe we are getting into something different; even that old mud bank over there is pretty low. Looks as though it ends up ahead there. What's that?"

A dull boom, like a distant cannon shot, from upstream. "D'you hear that?" Olaus yelled. We threw our utmost into pulling, peering upstream. "Be a good joke if we found people up here after thinking we were the only ones in creation."

"I don't think it sounded like rifle fire exactly."

"Could some party have come over from the Arctic? You said it was only about eighty miles in a straight line now."

We rounded the next bend. "Boom!" Right there, near us. Then Olaus shouted, pointing; ripples were running out against the current in one place. In the mud bank on the opposite shore we saw a great lens of dirty brown ice. We watched. Crash! A big piece of ice suddenly dropped into the water, a rending, a crash, and a splash. Here was the exact northern shore of that ancient lake; the Pleistocene ice was being defeated by summer sun and the modern stream.

Suddenly Jess threw up his arms with a shout: "She's clear!"

I dropped the line and rushed to the very edge; there on our side was clear, shining beautiful water. As though sighting a new planet, we looked down into the bottom, into the beautiful yellow gravel. Then we looked across, and halfway over, there was the dark line in the stream where the Pleistocene mud was still falling off with the ice. "Come on," Olaus shouted. "Let's get above that mud. Look, it's flattening out up here. We *are* in different country."

A mile above the lens of ice we made camp, to the accompaniment of that cannonading; it exploded regularly, every two minutes by the watch. We had, in the space of a few moments, emerged into another world. The gravel bank was low to the stream, flat as a floor, dotted with all manner of brave arctic bushes and flowers. Better yet, there was a breeze blowing, and best of all, we were on top of the world; we had come up out of weeks in that Pleistocene hole.

We threw off our head nets, gloves, and heavy shirts, and stood with the breeze blowing through our hair, gazing all around. We could see, far out over miles of green tundra, blue hills in the distance, on the Arctic coast no doubt. This was the high point; we had reached the headwaters of the Old Crow. After we had lived with it in all its moods, been down in the depths with it for weeks, it was good to know that the river began in beauty and flowed through miles of clean gravel and airy open space.

Latitude 68 degrees, 30 minutes.

We had a paradise camp for a few days. The men went out in the canoe and explored the river upstream. It became shallow rapidly, and they satisfied themselves that there were no other goose grounds. Martin had a heavenly time, turned loose in the air and sunshine. He had long since learned that gravel hurt his knees; he did not crawl, but walked on all fours like a cub bear. Here on a long leash he explored, crawling right over the low bushes, playing peek-a-boo behind them, scuttling away like a laughing rabbit when someone "found" him.

Jess caught some eighteen-inch grayling the very first night in the clear pools just above camp. The baby stood at my knee and kept begging for another bite and another bite while Jess kept saying: "It can't hurt him; it's good for him," till we realized he had consumed a whole big grayling.

Jess is a real fisherman, and getting these beauties, our first fish in weeks, lifted his spirits a little. But he was experiencing a letdown of sorts. He was drawing away from us, into himself. After all, I don't know how one could expect a trip of this kind to be all sweetness and light unless the personnel were recruited in heaven. Plenty of things could have affected Jess. Olaus and I were together; we were content; his Clara was miles, weeks, months, away from him, and she was to bear their sixth child in August before he could be with her again. Then his motorboat had let him down. Every one of those slow miles up the river since June 29 must have reminded him of how easy it all would have been with that engine. And now after the tremendous effort was over and we had reached the headwaters—well, there had to be a letdown.

It was hard having Jess lost to us. He became a polite stranger. At meals: "No thank you," instead of "Couldn't eat any more of the stuff!" "Yes, please," instead of "Hey, Mardy, you going to eat all the stew yourself?" He was even more polite to Olaus. They were really on the outs. Before, they had been two old pals on a trip together; now Jess was a stiffly polite employee; Olaus was the boss.

It was good that, while Olaus explored, Jess went fishing. I didn't blame him for needing to get away by himself.

Three days' respite from the mosquitoes; then it was time to turn south, back into the mud, and brown water, and clouds of insects. We all worked at sorting and reloading the outfit, in polite formality. The baby's little nook was placed amidships now, to make room up front for the rowing. The handmade oarlocks were put in place, then the two long oars, which had been made from two spruce trees.

On that last evening, after the baby was asleep, Olaus and I slipped across the river in the canoe and climbed up onto the tundra. It was ten o'clock, July 26. The sun had just slipped below a distant blue ridge, but bright saffron light filled the northwest; the rest was pale blue. It was still daytime, but that very still, strange exhilarating daytime of the arctic summer night, which can only be felt, not described. Here the flowing green-bronze tundra stretched as far as we could see—to the north, a few short ranges of hills; far to the south, rising pale blue off the flatness, the Old Crow Mountains again. In the morning we would be turning toward them.

We stood there for a long time, just looking. This might be our farthest north, ever. If we could only take a giant step and see the Arctic shore; we were so near.

Then our eyes came back to the near tundra, the velvety sphagnum hummocks, the myriad tiny arctic plants gleaming in the moss, in the golden light. The Labrador tea had gone to seed, but its sharp fragrance filled the air. In a tiny birch tree, a white-crowned sparrow, the voice of the arctic summer—"You will remember; you will remember," he sang.

JOHN MUIR

In Camp at Glacier Bay

JUNE 23. EARLY this morning we arrived in Glacier Bay. We passed through crowds of bergs at the mouth of the bay, though, owing to wind and tide, there were but few at the front of Muir Glacier. A fine, bright day, the last of a group of a week or two, as shown by the dryness of the sand along the shore and on the moraine—rare weather hereabouts. Most of the passengers went ashore and climbed the moraine on the east side to get a view of the glacier from a point a little higher than the top of the front wall. A few ventured on a mile or two farther. The day was delightful, and our one hundred and eighty passengers were happy, gazing at the

John Muir, the grandpa of environmental activism, spent his life waging a war to rescue the American West from turn-of-the-century industrialization. The Scottish-born Muir walked thousands of miles, recording the sights and sounds he knew would soon be lost. "In Camp at Glacier Bay" is from his 1890 journals.

beautiful blue of the bergs and shattered pinnacled crystal wall, awed by the thunder and commotion of the falling and rising icebergs, which ever and anon sent spray flying several hundred feet into the air and raised swells that set all the fleet of bergs in motion and roared up the beach, telling the story of the birth of every iceberg far and near. The number discharged varies much, influenced in part no doubt by the tides of weather and seasons, sometimes one every five minutes for half a day at a time on the average, though intervals of twenty or thirty minutes may occur without any considerable fall, then three or four immense discharges will take place in as many minutes. The sound they make is like heavy thunder, with a prolonged roar after deep thudding sounds—a perpetual thunderstorm easily heard three or four miles away. The roar in our tent and the shaking of the ground one or two miles distant from points of discharge seems startlingly near.

JUNE 25. A rainy day. For a few hours I kept count of the number of bergs discharged, then sauntered along the beach to the end of the crystal wall. A portion of the way is dangerous, the moraine bluff being capped by an overlying lobe of the glacier, which as it melts sends down boulders and fragments of ice, while the strip of sandy shore at high tide is only a few rods wide, leaving but little room to escape from the falling moraine material and the berg-waves. The view of the ice-cliffs, pinnacles, spires and ridges was very telling, a magnificent picture of nature's power and industry and love of beauty. About a hundred or a hundred and fifty feet from the shore a large stream issues from an arched, tunnel-like channel in the wall of the glacier, the blue of the ice hall being of an exquisite tone, contrasting with the strange, sooty, smoky, brown-colored stream. The front wall of the Muir Glacier is about two and a half or three miles wide. Only the central portion about two miles wide discharges icebergs. The two wings advanced over the washed and stratified moraine deposits have little or no motion, melting and receding as fast, or perhaps faster, than it advances. They have been advanced at least a mile over the old re-formed moraines, as is shown by the overlying, angular, recent moraine deposits, now being laid down, which are continuous with the medial moraines of the glacier.

In the old stratified moraine banks, trunks and branches of trees showing but little sign of decay occur at a height of about a hundred feet above tidewater. I have not yet compared this fossil wood with that of the opposite shore deposits. That the glacier was once withdrawn considerably back of its present limit seems plain. Immense torrents of water had filled in the inlet with stratified moraine-material, and for centuries favorable climatic conditions allowed forests to grow upon it. At length the glacier advanced, probably three or four miles, uprooting and burying the trees which had grown undisturbed for centuries. Then came a great thaw, which produced the flood that deposited the uprooted trees. Also the trees which grew around the shores above reach of floods were shed off, perhaps by the thawing of the soil that was resting on the buried margin of the glacier, left on its retreat and protected by a covering of moraine-material from melting as fast as the exposed surface of the glacier. What appears to be remnants of the margin of the glacier when it stood at a much higher level still exist on the left side and probably all along its bank on both sides just below its present terminus.

JUNE 30. CLEARING clouds and sunshine. In less than a minute I saw three large bergs born. First there is usually a preliminary thundering of comparatively small masses as the large mass begins to fall, then the grand crash and boom and reverberating roaring. Oftentimes three or four heavy main throbbing thuds and booming explosions are heard as the main mass falls in several pieces, and also secondary thuds and thunderings as the mass or masses plunge and rise again and again ere they come to rest. Seldom, if ever, do the towers, battlements, and pinnacles into which the front of the glacier is broken fall forward head-long from their bases like falling trees at the water-level or above or below it. They mostly sink vertically or nearly so, as if undermined by the melting action of the water of the inlet, occasionally maintaining their upright positions after sinking far below the level of the water, and rising again a hundred feet or more into the air with water streaming like hair down their sides from their crowns, then launch forward and fall flat with yet another thundering report, raising spray in magnificent, flamelike, radiating jets and sheets, occasionally to the very top of the front wall. Illumined by the sun, the spray and angular crystal masses are indescribably beautiful. Some of the discharges pour in fragments from clefts in the wall like waterfalls, white and mealy-looking, even dusty with minute swirling ice-particles, followed by a rushing succession of thunder-tones combining into a huge, blunt, solemn roar. Most of these crumbling discharges are from the excessively shattered central part of the ice-wall; the solid deep-blue masses from the ends of the wall forming the large bergs rise from the bottom of the glacier.

Many lesser reports are heard at a distance of a mile or more from the fall of pinnacles into crevasses or from the opening of new crevasses. The berg discharges are very irregular, from three to twenty-two an hour. On one rising ride, six hours, there were sixty bergs discharged, large enough to thunder and be heard at distances of from three quarters to one and a half miles; and on one succeeding falling tide, six hours, sixty-nine were discharged.

JULY 1. WE were awakened at four o'clock this morning by the whistle of the steamer George W. Elder. I went out on the moraine and waved my hand in salute and was answered by a toot from the whistle. Soon a party came ashore and asked if I was Professor Muir. The leader, Professor Harry Fielding Reid of Cleveland, Ohio, introduced himself and his companion, Mr. Cushing, also of Cleveland, and six or eight young students who had come well provided with instruments to study the glacier. They landed seven or eight tons of freight and pitched camp beside ours. I am delighted to have companions so congenial—we have now a village.

As I set out to climb the second mountain, three thousand feet high, on the east side of the glacier, I met many tourists returning from a walk on the smooth east margin of the glacier, and had to answer many questions. I had a hard climb, but wonderful views were developed and I sketched the glacier from this high point and most of its upper fountains.

Many fine alpine plants grew here, an anemone on the summit, two species of cassiope in shaggy mats, three or four dwarf willows, large blue hairy lupines eighteen inches high, parnassia, phlox, solidago, dandelion, white-flowered bryanthus, daisy, pedicularis, epilobium, etc., with grasses, sedges, mosses, and lichens, forming a delightful deep spongy sod. Woodchucks stood erect and piped dolefully for an hour "Chee-chee!" with jaws absurdly stretched to emit so thin a note— rusty-looking, seedy fellows, also a smaller striped species which stood erect and cheeped and whistled like a Douglas squirrel. I saw three or four species of birds. A finch flew from her nest at my feet; and I almost stepped on a family of young ptarmigan ere they scattered, little bunches of downy brown silk, small but able to run well. They scattered along a snow-bank, over boulders, through willows, grass, and flowers, while the mother, very lame, tumbled and sprawled at my feet. I stood still until the little ones began to peep; the mother answered "Too-too-too" and showed admirable judgment and devotion. She was in brown plumage with white on the wing primaries. She had fine grounds on which to lead and feed her young.

Not a cloud in the sky to-day; a faint film to the north vanished by noon, leaving all the sky full of soft, hazy light. The magnificent mountains around the widespread tributaries of the glacier; the great, gently undulating, prairie-like expanse of the main trunk, bluish on the east, pure white on the west and north; its trains of moraines in magnificent curving lines and many colors—black, gray, red, and brown; the stormy, cataract-like, crevassed sections; the hundred fountains; the lofty, pure white Fairweather Range; the thunder of the plunging bergs; the fleet of bergs sailing tranquilly in the inlet—formed a glowing picture of nature's beauty and power.

ROBERT COLES

Distances

THE ARCTIC COASTAL plain is flat, sandy, blessed with a network of lakes. The water is shallow. Sandbars and islands run parallel to a substantial stretch of the shore. Inland, the tundra seems limitless. The eyes are stopped only by an occasional clump of hemlocks, a burst of caribou, fast moving and soon enough out of sight. At about six or seven, certain Eskimo children ask their parents or schoolteachers whether the tundra ever ends. They are told about rivers that have their origins in mountain streams, about valleys that cut their way through rugged, uneven terrain. But they smile in disbelief—most of those stories Eskimo boys and girls

Robert Coles is a psychiatrist, teacher, and prolific author who has written over fifty books on topics ranging from Catholic Worker Dorothy Day to author James Agee, and from children's books to his own volumes of poetry. Coles won a Pulitzer Prize for his series from the 1980s, Children of Crisis. *"Distances" is from* The First and Last Eskimos *(1977).*

only gradually come to accept as "true," or as eminently suggestive as well as entertaining, intriguing. In the summer those children, and their parents, too, become preoccupied with what is near at hand: the thaw, which turns glacial gravels and permafrost into a lacework of turbid puddles; the wild flowers, in all sizes and colors; the profusion of grasses, thick and sometimes deep; the carpet of mosses and lichens, deep green or white or brown. But all of that, close by and for a while arresting, is no real match for the commanding presence of the sea, the tundra, the sky—the mystery of space, of distances.

An Eskimo youth, a young woman of fourteen who once spent half a year in Fairbanks, comments on the village life she lives, and the life she saw in the city, as well as the life she knows millions of her fellow Americans citizens take for granted: "I remember waking up in the house we had in Fairbanks; I went to the window, and I saw—another house. I bent my neck and looked, and there was the sky, a small piece of it—the size of fish or meat we have in the middle of the winter, not fish or meat we eat in the summer! Everywhere we went there were houses and stores. We kept looking at walls. I couldn't see beyond a street; there were always cars and buildings. The sky was not the same sky I knew. There was no ocean. At school there was a playground, but across the street there were stores. My mother said she felt a lot of time as if she wasn't getting enough air inside her. My father ended up in the bars at night, drinking. He didn't see anything except the beer inside a bottle.

"One day he came home and said he wanted to go back to our village; he wanted to stand near the ocean and look at the water, not drown in beer. We left the next day. My uncle has been in Fairbanks for a long time, but my father couldn't stay, and I'm glad we're back here. As soon as we got home, my grandmother told me to go say hello to the ocean, and to the ponds, and to take a walk through the grass, and to watch for foxes and say hello to them. And not to forget the sky; she never does—she's always looking at the sky and watching the clouds, and she can tell if the weather will change by the way the clouds go across the sky. She won't tell me her secret. She says I'll learn it by looking long enough myself!"

She does that; she looks and looks. She looks closely at flowers nearby, the short stems, the heavy blossoms. She looks closely at the snow—soft and clumpy, or crusty, or shimmering in its subtle lines, currents, and crosscurrents. She gazes—a mix of attention directed outward and a meditative mood. She scans the horizon, or the flocks of ducks, geese, birds: wither and with what dispatch and how many? She stares fixedly— the movements of a dog, a fox, a bird hold her in apparent thralldom, as she herself seems to realize: "I can't take my eyes off a duck sometimes. I pick one, and I follow it, until it lets me go—by flying far enough away. Then I am free to go away myself: I'm back looking at the clouds, and trying to see if they are running or walking, and if they bring summer rain or just themselves, with the sun melting them every once in a while.

"If you look far enough away, you see the point where the sky and the land join; that is where I would like to go. My father says you can never get there, because there is always a point, far away, where the sky and the land join! Maybe that is why the caribou herds keep running all over; they are trying to find that place! They must be looking for something; otherwise, they would stay still more, or only move when they see us. But I've watched them when they haven't seen me, and they keep going, going. I'm sure they are looking for a home—and it must be at that place where the sky and the land touch each other; then there wouldn't be anyplace farther to go. As long as there is more land to see, and a sky to look at, the caribou decide to keep moving. They must get tired every once in a while. They must close their eyes and stop staring out at the land and the sky."

She constantly refers to vision, to the subtleties of sight; and in so doing, she indicates what obtains her interest—the vast landscape, part of which she stands on, part of which she stands under, and part of which, she knows, enables her and others to stay alive. The last, the sea, is nourishing to her, but mystifying, too. She runs to the sea when she is unhappy—only, at times, to run away, toward land, because she is not quite soothed, and maybe made troubled afresh. Her life is a matter of balancing horizons—that of the water, that of the land, that of the air. She has been told since she was a young girl that she would have to learn to do so. She was told through stories, whose moral or instructional implications were not missed by her and the other grandchildren who listened: "My grandmother used to tell us we must all come listen to her. So, we did. She would point to the ocean, and tell us we must never forget its seals and fish and whales—our food. She would point to the land, and tell us that we are, all the time, guests of the land. We walk on it, and sit on it, and run on it, and our houses are on it, and our food—the caribou—are also its guests. She would point to the sky, and remind us that the sky brings us water, and brings us air, and the light of the summer.

"She would tell us how our people have kept alive all these years: we haven't forgotten the sky and the land and the ocean. My grandmother bows to the ocean, and to the sky and to the land every morning. She doesn't like bowing to the cross in church; she says the church is too small, and the cross is too big. She asked the priest why we don't pray outside in the summer. He said a church is a place you go inside—to speak with God. My grandmother says God is in the ocean, and in the sky, and under the ground. We can never see Him, but He is there, way off in the distance. You should look, she said, very hard—because He'll know you're trying to see Him, and when you go to sleep and die He'll remember you were thinking of Him."

She remembers times when she thinks she may have elicited a pre-burial day response from Him. She has found herself taking walks, or simply standing on a slight turn upward of the land, when, all of a sudden, the world around her seems responsive to her. She does not, afterward, say that such was the case. She never moves from the tentative to the convinced. But she has felt herself in the presence of a watchful, heedful universe, and the result has been a touch of awe, a moment of perplexed acquiescence—as if she can't quite believe what she has seen or heard and found so significant. She makes, finally, no effort to "resolve" her mystical side and her practical side, her Eskimo side and her American-educated side. She simply recalls how it went for her: "I walked to the ocean because I felt sick. My mother sends us to the ocean when we get sick. I had a pain in my belly. The teachers tell you to have a Coke, or milk. My mother says to take a walk, and look at the water, and way off, the ice. I did. I forgot about the pain. I got lost—in the ice. I pictured myself riding on a moving pack of ice. The next thing I knew, the wind came up; I felt it right on my face, strong. I guess I was brought back to shore by the wind!

"When I look way out, across the water, I am sure there is somebody there who sees me. God? I don't know. Maybe my grandmother was wrong. Maybe no one is there! Sometimes I stare at the sky, and watch the clouds in the summer, and suddenly they all scatter, and the sun is staring back at me! I don't just look away. I lower my head, then I turn toward the ocean. Maybe the sun doesn't like me trying to figure out what the weather will be. The teacher says in the lower forty-eight they have machines to predict the weather. In the naval station they have those machines—down the coast. But the sun fools them, and the clouds.

"I'll be running, and I kick up some land. I keep running. I kick up more land. Then I fall—a hole in the ground. I always feel I've been punished. The teachers send you out of the classroom; my grandmother

warns you with a story; the land decides to trick you and make you stumble. I can swear I see a shadow, way off in the distance, when I get up. I
can swear there is a reason for falling; my grandmother says there is a reason. The soil has been kicked by my feet. I'll get in trouble. I can feel the
'ouch' coming from the ground. I might stop and try to put everything
back in its place, or I might run even faster. Either way, I'll catch it later;
I'll usually stumble. Or I'll see darkness ahead—a black cloud so far off it
seems to be coming out of the land, not down from the sky. Then it's time
to turn around and go home."

When she is back home she turns around again, looks again. She
has an intent, wandering, searching pair of eyes. She seems to be wondering whether someone, something, has been following her—spirits,
ghosts, one of those saints the priest talks about, maybe God Almighty
Himself. They are all off there, in the distance—so she believes. The
world ends—or begins—a step or two outside of the settlement she
belongs to, a rather finite and circumscribed collection of houses, with a
small store and a small school. There is nothing, really, between her community and any others in Alaska—no roads or railroad tracks or even
pathways to connect one group of people to another. She and her cousins
and friends don't make reference to other places, even neighboring villages—meaning a place fifty miles or one hundred miles away. Life is
directed at survival from day to day—though a plane once a week does
bring in mail and provisions.

Children as well as old people (the latter remember a time when
no plane came, and when it was successful hunting and fishing, or starva-
tion) regard the settlement as a spot in a stretch of infinity, a lone star in a
sky whose mysteries are very much beyond everyone's reach, though (as
always) there are plenty of explanations and theories around. Teachers
have their maps, with mileages; the priest, his Bible and conviction that

God is, to say the least, immanent and transcendent both—not unmindful of anyone, anywhere. But the girl looks up or straight outward—and feels removed in space (and, maybe, time) from just about everyone and everything. She also feels, has been taught to feel, vulnerable as well as self-reliant; "A strong wind, and we suffer. We have to be prepared to be alone all winter. The plane may not come for weeks and weeks. It is us against the sea and the sky and the land; they send snow and wind and the worst cold against us, and we have to be strong. When I was small I remember asking my mother why the weather came from someplace—and there was probably trouble there, and that's why we get trouble here. But she wasn't sure what kind of trouble. My grandfather said he knew—the fights our ancestors had with other people keep going on, and they cause the storms we get here."

She remembers as a younger child standing beside her grandfather. He held her hand tightly. He told her to stare out across the tundra, not to blink, not to look away. If she did so, bowed her head or closed her eyes for any noticeable length of time, he told her why it was important for her to stand fast—with her head, her eyes, as well as her body. There are spirits waiting, watching, or alas, venting their spleens, way over "there"—across the frozen soil and across the ice-covered sea, or across the water temporarily unlocked from winter's bondage, or beyond the visible sky. There is only one way Eskimos have learned to endure; they know to face up to extreme danger, to face down nature's unpredictable assaults. If a child is going to become, one day, a sturdy, tough-minded, inventive, and persevering hunter or fisherman, or a mother who gives hope to children in the face of the fiercest, most unyielding storms, then there is no better way to learn than on the shore's edge when a strong gust comes up, or amid the grasses of the tundra when the clouds gather ominously and the temperature falls, falls, and the snow begins to come down with a thickness and speed—all of which indicates that the summer is over, the light will slowly go away, and (as some Eskimos believe) the distant horizon will disappear.

The young woman explains how that last phenomenon happens, and why: "During the summer we have been allowed to look far, far away. There is light all the time, and we can see over to the islands and beyond them, and way inland, past several ponds. And there are no clouds a lot of the time, and we see the entire sky and the sun. Then winter comes, and we get to see very little. There is nothing far away to see. We are lucky to be able to walk to a friend's house and get there in the dark—against the heavy snow. The sea gets covered and so does the land, and so does the sky: ice, snow, and clouds. In the winter my grandfather used to tell me it's all right to close your eyes and not even try to look outside. The harder you try to see, the less you do see because your eyes begin to go blind with fear!"

That said, she closes her eyes for a moment—even though it is now midsummer. But they are soon enough open, and she is looking across the bay at her favorite sight, place, spot: a cone-shaped rock that juts out of the water—a resting place for sea gulls. Those gulls have always meant a lot to her, maybe too much, she says. Her mother once told her to stop paying so much attention to sea gulls. She obeyed—or seemed to. She became a more covert observer of them. She came to believe that she had in her a sea gull's temperament, if not "spirit." She has spent minutes watching them, perched on that rock, watch the world. She observes them observing the Arctic coast from the air. She envies them for the grace of their carriage while flying. But she especially pays attention to them when they land on the rock. Then, for her, they are kindred souls. Then, for her, the distance between that rock and the shore becomes inconsequential.

She has them meditating as she does—thinking about the various Arctic scenes and trying to make some sense of things: "I wonder if the sea gulls see me. I've tried moving, to see if they would move. But they know the difference between near and far! If they were on the shore, here, and saw me move, they would fly away. Even here, they keep an eye on you, and if you're not too near, they'll stay on their feet, but watch you all the time. It's got so that I know if I take one more step, they'll fly off. The teacher says I should figure out the exact distance and keep testing the gulls, and then I'd be a scientist, and I'd have my proof—so many yards, and the birds take off! But I don't want to know how many yards. I want to play games, I guess! I can see them playing games with me; and they always win.

"Once, a gull let me come closer than ever before. I couldn't believe it! I thought I'd be able to touch it. I thought it was in trouble—the wings didn't work. I kept moving nearer and nearer. All of a sudden the gull took off. I can hear its wings going, right now, in my ears! I'll never forget the noise—like waves, hitting the rocks. The gull didn't fly away; it flew right over me, back and forth. I saw its eyes, and it saw mine! I think it was trying to figure out what kind of Eskimo I am! It kept circling me. I decided to walk. The gull followed me. I was sure it was trying to be friendly. Then it landed, way up the shore. I ran toward it, and it flew away, out toward the rock. I think I scared it when I ran.

"My father always tells me that the distance between us and an animal or a bird or a fish is very important. If you're going to catch something, you have to figure out how near you can come. You have to know how far the bullet will go, and how far the line will stretch. You can't chase a bird; you can creep up on it, but you have to be very slow and patient. When you run, you're wasting your time. I've chased sea gulls, but that's having fun with them. If I want to get close to them, I take a step, and count to ten, and then another. But I've never got as close to a sea gull as I did that one time. My grandmother says the gull might 'know' me. Maybe an Eskimo's spirit is in the gull!"

At other times she leaves the shore, walks inland, kneels down and admires the summer flowers—a poppy, some Arctic cotton. She especially likes to look at the land when the snow has first fallen, or when it has melted down, but not disappeared. She notices patterns, designs, lines and circles of white that cover the tundra. She likes to make her own lines and circles, too—sketches of sorts on the snow. Her ears are as sensitive as her eyes. She listens to the gulls, hears the wind working its way through the shrubs, plants, man-made nets or lines. She walks up to the drying salmon in the late summer and smells the fish, touches the fish, steps back and watches a beam of sun on the pink-red of the fish. She moves back, savors the fish again, now from a small distance; she reminds herself how full her stomach is, how relatively empty it will be in midwinter, when severe and repeated storms can jeopardize even a carefully stocked supply of provisions. She sits and watches the sun, falling late at night over the ocean— the strange pink color against the distant ice floes, the uncanny mixture of light and dark. And in winter she notices the blue color of the air: enough light to take the edge off the blackness, but not enough to let the color of things really stand out.

In the summer she has stood transfixed, it seems, by the sight of a boat out in the ocean. She hopes the boat will move in closer, but knows it will not. It is on its way to a harbor farther up the coast. Yet, for some reason, it has stopped, is biding its time. She wonders why—wonders whether the Eskimos would be alive today were it not for boats like that, and the planes that fly overhead, and the canned goods she has come to accept as inevitable, as helpful indeed. She has put the question to her grandparents, and heard their answer: "My grandfather said that we were here long before the white people and their planes and ships. My grandmother took me to the fish she has stored. She took me to the skins, hanging. She showed me the meat. She said I am going to school, and that's my trouble! She's not against the Eskimo's going to school; she just wants us to remember that the teachers should come see us, and take lessons from us. They spend a lot of time making sure they're all right until the next plane lands. We don't have to worry about the next plane."

It is a distance from her house to the school. She goes back and forth, literally and spiritually. She admires the tough, independent, self-sufficient ways of her parents and grandparents, yet has not failed to notice that they have stoves, pots and pans, canned goods—and recently, a snowmobile. She remembers when that last phenomenon first arrived in her community. She was excited by the machine—the strong, assertive noise, the colors, the complicated machinery, and not lease, the effortless speed. The dogs were jealous, she was convinced. She was jealous—such an immediate and gratifying capacity to overcome distance, "destroy the space." That is what she said one day about the snowmobile: "It gets you from here to anywhere in a few seconds. There's no space left; you just get inside, and the machine goes, and you sit there and watch the land go by, and there's nothing left between you and any place. You destroy the space."

She treasures that space, those distances she has come to find so much a part of her life. She has not stopped taking rides on the snowmobile; has not ceased enjoying herself, feeling the thrill one might expect a person of her age, especially, to acknowledge. But she can get out, after laughing, even shrieking with apparent joy, and look gratefully across the tundra, or out toward the sea. No matter how fast that snowmobile goes, and no matter how promptly she gets taken in it from this place to that one, there are still farther distances—to the point, she knows, that the immense, boundless Arctic is more than a match for those roaring, cocky motors that belong to those boastfully painted metal bodies.

Acknowledgments

Introduction Michael Doogan ©1993 by Michael Doogan.

"The Encircled River" from *Coming into the Country* by John McPhee ©1985 by John McPhee. Reprinted by permission of Farrar Straus Giroux.

Excerpt from *Tracks Across Alaska* by Alastair Scott ©1990 by Alastair Scott. Reprinted by permission of Atlantic Monthly Press.

Excerpt from *The Eskimo Storyteller* by Edwin S. Hall ©1975 by the University of Tennessee. Reprinted by permission of the University of Tennessee.

"The Young Men and the Sea" by Larry Gallagher ©1990 by Larry Gallagher. Reprinted by permission of the author.

Excerpt from *Dead in the Water* by Dana Stabenow ©1993 by Dana Stabenow. Reprinted by permission of Berkely Books.

Excerpt from *A Pioneer Woman in Alaska* by Emily Craig Romig ©1954 by Emily Craig Romig. Reprinted by permission of the author.

Excerpts from *Alaskans: Life on the Last Frontier*, edited by Ron Strickland ©1992 by Stackpole Books. Reprinted by permission of Stackpole Books.

"Geese" from *Two in the Far North* by Margaret Murie ©1978 by Margaret Murie. Reprinted by permission of the Alaska Northwest Publishing Company.

"Distances" from *The First and Last Eskimos* by Robert Coles ©1978 by by Robert Coles. Reprinted by permission of New York Graphic Society.